Smooth
Hard

L.I. ter Meulen

True North Press, LLC

True North Press, LLC

ISBN: 978-0-578-25587-3

Library of Congress Control Number: 2021921826

Cover Photo © 2022 www.gettyimages.com. All rights reserved - used with permission.

PRINTED IN THE UNITED STATES OF AMERICA

"I am fonder of my past now than
I was when it was my present."
Anonymous

In Memory of Jeffrey Escoffier

Dedicated to Bertha Harris

EPISODE ONE

Emily

My mother's affairs are episodic and come in waves. Her weakness is "real men," men who outwardly display the best of the male traits. Virile. Vocal. Confident. Alec, my father, was the enigmatic other. Fluid. Mercurial. Mysterious. But he is also the male cornerstone. The other lovers of her life rest upon her memories of her year with Alec. There are occasions between and during her romantic episodes when I see her gazing at and stroking that smooth polished stone from a beach in Nice, her talisman.

As a child I am fascinated with the story of Alec and my mother. It is, after all, the story of how I came into existence, who I am becoming. I especially love the telling of how they met. My mother, the pragmatic, the practical, falling utterly in love "at first sight," as she described it. Totally for the only time in her life, and with a very unsuitable lover. What a complicated coupling to be borne of. I suppose we all are. I yearn for more of my own life, apart from hers. The desire to understand her and her dynamic with men -- and the way all the generations of men and women before me loved and fought together -- grows more urgent, especially as I become a woman. So I continue to press her for more information, more detail. I want to know the silent, staring steps that led up to the day they met, as if it were a nursery tale that must be followed exactly word by word, and if a single word is left out the entire meaning of the story and the ending itself will change.

Maybe that's the reason Mom is so reluctant to tell the whole story. If a single word changes or one step is left out, all the rest of history and her life will be altered forever.

After Alec, my father, whom I know only through my mother's (at first) terse and (then) exuberant answers, and a few photos, there is Cyril. Tall, reedy, and elegant, and jealously abusive. Then Jim, handsome, debonair, and embracing, and curiously soft at the core. And then Barry, daring and adventurous on the surface, yet privately nervous and hand-wringing. And all the others in between whose names and faces are a blur.

The only conclusion I reach, watching and analyzing these men as I grow alongside my mother's love life, is that "real men" come bundled with a significant reservoir of insecurities. In relating to me, they always work hard to impress me, like cowboys doing lasso tricks or shooting cans in the air. I am small, tough, and cynical at an early age. I am not an easy audience.

I don't know myself entirely. I know only the side of me that reflects my mother, Jante – *Jantay* -- round-faced, pretty, and a little pudgy. And yes, her real name is Janet, -altered by her venture in France where I was conceived. Unlike her even-tempered reticence, I bear a wild streak that always makes me wonder about my father. Mother has a perpetual attachment to him, though she hasn't talked to him since she left him in France shortly after my conception. All the while I am growing up, I prod my mother to tell me their story. I am interested in sex at an implausibly early age. I begin self-pleasuring when I am five, and playing doctor at every opportunity. I hope their story involves a lot of sex, and I try to innocently probe her about this.

"When did you meet Alec?"

"It was summer." As I get older, Mom gets bolder

in her responses and embellishes the simple answers of my early childhood. When I turn thirteen, she adds, "I always think of summer when I think of Alec. I always associate him with the sultry and exotic."

"Where did you meet him?"

"He was serving cold drinks in a café on the Promenade, across from the Sporting Plage." Mom always pauses for a brief moment here and looks me in the eye while I blink innocently and even hold my breath a little until she continues. "I knew the moment our eyes met that something would happen between us." I love that line, "something would happen," and spend hours imagining what that could be.

"What's the Sporting Plage?"

"It's a private beach in Nice where handsome young busboys serve you ice cream and drinks while you sun bathe…"

"Can we go there..?"

"Sure…"

"When? Was it love at first sight…?"

"The only time in my life …"

"Then what happened?"

"Nothing." My mother answers with her "it's not that important" shrug, before continuing, "it was like that for four, five maybe six weeks. Every day I walked into his cafe and ordered a cold drink." At thirteen, just as my own hormones are bubbling to the surface, she enhances the story: "And his brown eyes would burn into me while pretending to be engrossed in the act of drawing cool liquids into a tall, chilled glass, just for me, of course." She is a writer, after all, and missed her calling: pulp fiction.

"And then what?" I ask, blinking innocently.

"One day I gave him my business card."

"And?"

"And, well, he looked at it briefly before putting it into his pocket..." When I am fifteen she adds, "A little smile came to rest at the edge of his mouth and I think he wondered why had I waited so long." And she is a hapless romantic. I just want her to get to the good part. By this time in my own life, I feel I've gone farther in a few hours than my parents did those first six weeks.

She gives me the photos from that summer. They are worn at the edges and faded.

"This is my favorite picture of Alec." The old photos may have faded, but his handsome looks are beguiling. He is not too tall, with a narrow frame. Beneath his white shirt, his chest is nearly bare of hair except for a small boyish tuft in the center left, over his heart. When I am sixteen, she ruminates dreamily, "I can still remember sifting my fingers through his hair and holding onto it when he would slip into sleep beside me."

His eyes look away from the camera, as if watching for someone to come down the road to meet him.

"Was it love at first sight?"

"Oh yes. At least for me."

How did you know?" This is what I always ask, and then she tells me how their eyes met the first time.

How old were you?

"I was 30. I think he was in his twenties when we met. I never was exactly sure how old Alec was. He was very guarded."

Was he in love with you?

Mother lets out a little strangled, "Hhhhhm, who knows? I thought so. Then he wasn't. I'm not sure he was ever in love with anyone besides himself."

When I am little and ask too many questions at any one time, she'd give me a little pat on my behind to send me off. "You're the curious one, aren't you?" When I am older, she begins to write me answers that often sound more like short stories.

As soon as my childhood is cleaved by the deep sharp blade, the great divide known as adolescence, I am fairly free-roaming. My mother is decidedly not curious about my love life, and maybe she is just afraid to ask. I experiment widely and love the freedom of not having to talk to her about it. Sometimes I wish I had an adult to talk to, but I am reluctant to cross that bridge with my mother. She does, though, discreetly leave a box of condoms in my medicine chest for my sixteenth birthday. A variety pack: tingling sensation "for her," flavored, and plain.

But as my blossoming hormones surge, my questions become more nuanced, more personal. A little pushy. Did you have fun together? Did you see other men? Were there other women?

As I am discovering the uncertain terrain of sexual activity in my own life the one question I always want to ask is "Did you have orgasms with him?" But I don't have the nerve.

Before I am seventeen, Mom begins to open up. "I was flattered at our affair. There was really no reason for me to be, since Alec was prolific, and with both men and women he was indiscriminate. He was a sensationalist." New word for my vocabulary. I like the sound of it and start using it at school to describe myself.

And by the time I am eighteen there is no stopping her.

"I don't know if Alec really needed to have frequent sex with a lot of people, or if he was afraid of missing out on something, anything, that life offered. And sex offers such an easy fast route to sensation.

(As if I didn't know.)

"The truth is I was so in love with Alec, I thought we were Adam and Eve and no other love affair ever existed in the universe. That's how silly I was at the moment. And to this day I do believe that Alec was, in his own way, at least, loving me; I have come to realize his way was more nuanced, more sophisticated. And yet I have always believed, always needed to believe it was so, that Alec also wanted our innocence to be real, and true."

And, of course, the question that is never satisfactorily answered in the minds of the offspring of divorced parents: "Why did you leave him?" And, "Why are you always so reluctant to talk about Alec?" I've always thought of my father as Alec, never as Dad, or Daddy. After all, I'd never met him; he never knew I existed. When I refer to him with my friends, he is transformed into My Father, Alexandro.

Jante's response to her past is, "It's like flotsam. I was young. It's embarrassing and sordid to be young." She loves her sea analogies. And she is such a novelist, especially when she is drinking. Unlike you are now -- mature, sane, thoughtful. Thanks, Mom.

"But it's Alec's story you want to hear; after all, I can hide my own mistakes in the shadows of his. And it isn't as if Alec was ever silly. On the contrary. Locked inside his easygoing exterior, he was very serious."

That night I find a note from Mom under my pillow; her way of sharing second thoughts with me or sometimes just her philosophy about life. Though she has a knack for embellishment after a few glasses of wine, she isn't really much of a storyteller. She is more like a reporter's fact sheet. I watch her story unfold before me, her love affairs, her gripes, her struggle with addictions: to men, too much wine, work. She struggled as a writer, starting as a travel writer, which took her to France in the first place, where she met Alec, my father, and then kept us afloat with magazine articles. One time she even wrote an article on 'Finding True Love on Vacation in the South of France.' Ironic, I thought, she is now the authority? Since then I've been skeptical about so-called "experts" in magazines.

Her note that night is more philosophical than factual.

"Em. Perhaps this is why I have avoided the story. Reliving the past reminds me so much of all I have missed. The lost opportunities, the moments I might have lived differently, taken a different path, made everything turn out the way I really thought it ought to. Then again, how many of us ever really think much about what our lives ought to be? We are just too busy sorting out what it is at the moment. Why do we worry about the future, and regret the past? To avoid recognizing the stark aloneness, the sheer precariousness of the present moment.

"Facing the beauty and terror of it, how do we dare

believe or hope for another moment, how can we bear the fear? In it, that ever fleeing creature we call Now, we are a period, an exclamation point, a comma, in the story of our own life, a story always unfolding, surprising. Only the past remains perfect, told, unchangeable, and safe from our future mistakes.

"It's not that the memories are so painful. And it's not that I don't want to remember Alec -- he's in my thoughts always, I never forget him -- it's just that it is simpler living in the present, stepping forever into the next moment than it is to look back, trying to retrieve the past. Like I said, it's like flotsam."

Despite her love of evidence, sometimes is like digging into wet sand to get the facts from my mother.

EPISODE TWO

Jante's Diary

"Emily, dear. I know how curious you are about your father, Alec. Perhaps one day we'll look him up and you can meet him for yourself! Though he will be surprised. I never told him I was pregnant with his child. But I have never forgotten him; he is very much alive for me; that year I spent with him lives on inside me. And now in you.

"You also know that I don't speak easily, that writing a narrative comes more easily to me than talking openly about my past, or my feelings. So, here is a story, for your birthday. It is the story of how you came to be, seventeen years ago! But more than that, it will (I hope) answer all your questions about the relationship between your father and me. (Maybe you'll stop asking, hint, hint!) We met in Nice. I was a travel writer, a dream job. Living and being paid to write about the Riviera.

I love you, happy reading,

Mom.

P.S. I've included a photo. I love this picture of Alec. It is my favorite way of remembering him. It makes me melancholy. [In the photo a young, tousled Alec is standing, leaning aloofly, looking away from the rest of his friends.]

Nice, Côte d'Azur

Over time, Alec's rough edge will become a polished plane that will keep the world at cool abeyance. It's a surface that over the years Alec methodically and quietly sanded and fingered until the rough edge became a solid, detached veneer. When I met him, his roughness was an integral aspect of his attractiveness to both sexes. Everyone wants to rub up against him as a cat would against a scratchy surface. Within a year, the edge will be smoothed out all over and he will be like alabaster.

The first time I look at Alec, I see a fire inside his bittersweet chestnut eyes. I wonder if this man whose glance burns into me isn't in fact dangerous, and decide he isn't dangerous, but probably very mischievous, and most definitely erotic.

After a few weeks, looking at him, desiring him, I give him my business card. He calls me late that afternoon and suggests we meet me at the Splendid Hotel. Even though I still think he might be dangerous, I meet him there. We have great sex, and he says he loves me. He falls asleep, but I lie awake and stare at him through the dark, unbelieving, startled to find such a pretty man in bed with me.

After that first night, I am eager to introduce Alec to my friends. I want everyone to know that I'd (at last!) caught a handsome fish. I plan on guarding my catch zealously. I had for a long while been viewed as a single girl. Everyone tells me I am attractive, with pretty skin, nice hands, a pleasing face and soft figure. A little chubby, but soft. And no boyfriend. I date only occasionally; I am bored easily with men, and as my fascination with them ends, so does theirs with me. I have learned how essential a woman's interest is in men who haven't formed themselves into anything yet, and sadly, even more so for mature men who have.

The next night, I make plans to meet Alec at Club le Cirque and decide to arrive a little late, foolishly confident that Alec will grow anxious while waiting for me. I suppose every love affair weighs in with its own little checks and balances: who is anxious and who isn't. I'm wearing my pale-green dress, the one that shows off my tan.

The place is a crowd of faces mostly unfamiliar to me. I see the bar, but Alec isn't there, and am grateful when Jack grabs my elbow and sways me around to meet his newest girlfriend. Jack is one of my failed dates, and yet he treats me kindly, as if I am an old friend.

"Michelle, here is a grand woman who almost broke my heart and could have! But she was kind enough to warn me off her rocky shoals before our first date even ended..." So that's how they see me, the opposite of a siren.

"I think it was before our first -- and last -- date even got started. And Jack is too generous; he's the one who lost interest even before our second drink."

Michelle is a pretty, bland girl who layers on just the right amount of attentive gazing on Jack; she laughs approvingly at everything Jack says. It is so easy to know just the right thing to say to new girlfriends. Just don't plan any serious conversations. She will probably hold on to him for a long time.

"Are you here alone...?"

Jack notices my restless peering about. Usually he wouldn't even think to ask, since I always am.

"Well, I am meeting someone..."

"Hey, speaking of meeting someone, there's someone here tonight I want you to meet --- I'm surprised to

14

find him here; this isn't really his sort of place. I think you'll like him."

The wonderful thing about unsuccessful first dates that you run into, especially after they have a new girl-friend, is how willing they are to find you another date.

"Where's Wiley and crew?"

At that moment I see Alec, though not as I had imagined him, waiting nervously at the bar for my arrival. Just cool and aloof. My heart beats faster and my mouth gets dry when I see him.

"They drove to Marseille for the weekend; they made plans last night, I guess you weren't around or..."

"No. No, I was busy."

When Alec sees me, he doesn't smile. I even momentarily detect a slight embarrassment. I blush. I am to discover that Alec never blushes, and often doesn't smile, except when it serves a purpose. I think he is incapable of obvious displays of human weakness, and soon I come to realize that the rough edge is being worked on, and eventually will be all ironed out, obscuring a natural response that might result in a blush. Or a natural smile.

The moment Alec and I lock eyes, Jack spies Alec and says, "Ah, here's the good-looking guy I want you to meet, Alec. I hear he's a great lover..."

Hear? Hear from who? This is a question I would have asked if I had been more attuned to the moment, instead of being totally, indiscreetly in love vaulting into the future as Mrs. Alexandro, fleeing my past awkward aloneness. This occurs to me only subliminally, later, when I can't be sure that it had happened at all.

"We've met."

EPISODE THREE

Jante and Alec

After a few months, Alec and I become a "couple" -- that is, other people expect to see us together, and if we aren't together ask each of us about the other when there is a lull in conversation. I suppose, in retrospect, I took on the role of girlfriend with a deeper sense of responsibility than Alec did his as a boyfriend. I was older, it's true, and a woman. Women usually do take these things more seriously than men do. But we are spending a lot of time together, most nights, and I take that as a sign of something meaningful. Everyone calls him Alex, except me.

"As soon as the deal comes through with my uncle, I'm quitting the café." A soda engineer. That's how he describes his job at the café. "The deal" with Uncle Eduardo sounds like a winning lottery ticket. Eduardo lives in Barcelona, where Alec grew up, with his older brother, Alec's father Esteban.

"I hate waiting on people," he said.

"You're not a good servant," I concede.

He rolls his eyes. "So true."

"But you have to make a living."

He sighs. "So true."

For myself, I'd imagined I was going to have a great fling with a rich and spoiled Playboy of the West, cavorting in the South of France on the back of his motorcycle along the Grande Corniche on our way to Monaco, the gorgeous sea spread out below us and the wind blowing madly through my hair, and me serene as a queen.

With Alec, well, the playboy part comes true. The nights when he doesn't show up make me crazy, but I accept this side of the equation. He is the most stirring man I've ever met, and he makes my heart race.

We spend more time in the company of his friends than we do alone, and Alec never speaks of his family except to mention "the deal" with his uncle. One night, we are together after having spent a rare afternoon alone with each other. A semi-sweet afternoon;

18

Alec is more relaxed, almost pensive at times, seeking some sort of answer at a point in the horizon that I can't see. It is rare that Alec is not preening or staging himself in some way for others' viewing. He is, in fact, more himself this one day than I have ever seen him before, and that allows me to relax, too.

In the dark that night, he speaks quietly. "You know the uncle I talk about?"

"The one with the deal?"

"Yes. Eduardo. Eduardo has taught me many things. I remember Eduardo walking me along the Barcoleneta when I was fourteen, smiling and bare-chested. He nudged me, 'Look at that woman, she puts her hand to her heart when she sees you, she's old enough to be your grandmother and her tongue is almost hanging to her toes. She'd pay good money for you.' I felt very proud of myself. I wanted everyone on the beach to run over and give me money. It excited me. Money and sex. Of course, I was just bait. I later discovered Eduardo himself made out like a bandit with abuela." He chuckles. "Eduardo had his ways with women"

"What does he look like?"

"Honestly? He looks like a French ditch digger, though he is more of a gold digger. Women are just drawn to him. His mannerisms, I guess-- masculine, he has strong arms and always a little unshaven. I always wanted to be like him."

"And your father?"

"Esteban. He's quiet. Reserved. Better looking than Eduardo. But do you know? I think Eduardo might be my father. At least that's what I think my mother always believed. My mother was in love with Eduardo."

I say nothing, just lie alongside Alec in the dark. Is more coming? When he doesn't say anything, I ask, "What is your mother like?"

"Was. Was. She's dead. Gisele."

Alec was quiet again, then, in a murmured child-like voice I barely recognize as Alec's he adds, "She was pretty." A pause and then his manly voice again, "And confused."

I listen.

"I think she killed herself."

I don't say anything; what can I say?

"She was especially agitated that day. I was always nervous when she was like that -- too giddy, too much on the edge. I never knew how she would act when she was like that, whether she was going to laugh or cry, as if it was all mixed up inside her. Sometimes she would just buy me things, ice cream and candy, and then she'd hit me if I got too excited with her and ... well, she was more and more often like that.

"She and my father and my uncle had gone out the night before. My father came home early to put me to bed. She came in later, much later. I heard her arguing with my father; then they were quiet. In the morning she came into the kitchen while I was having toast. My father, Esteban, always fixed me toast in the morning and then she'd walk me to school. Her eyes were red, and she drank a lot of coffee. She just left me at the door to my school and she waved and smiled her wild edgy smile and stepped off the curb and..."

His breath is shallow.

"The driver said she looked him directly in the eye before stepping into the street..."

"Alec. I am sorry." I place my hand on his chest and gently grab the boyish hairs there. "I'm sorry." He shrugs and pushes my hand away.

A shadow seems to rise out of Alec's chest and sit there before filling the whole room with a dark sadness. He turns his back to me. By morning, the heavy weight dissipates, and he is his mischievously moody, rough around the edges self again.

The next afternoon, when I feel the sadness is safely squirreled away, I ask Alec why his mother had married his father if she was in love with his uncle.

"My father is the stable one. He always held a steady job, he has worked all his life and now holds a pension. My uncle is the opposite. He can't be relied on to support a family. And she met Esteban first."

"Can Eduardo be relied on to make deals?" I realize

21

as soon as I say this that I struck a sensitive cord. Alec winces and curtly answers, "Yes," but I can see a shadow of doubt in his glance away from me.

"After the deal" prefaces most of our plans and conversations early that summer. We sit on the rail gazing at the Mediterranean over the sea of blue and white umbrellas shielding the tourists lounging in supreme comfort at the private beaches. Alec will say, "After the deal we're all going to rent chaises and mattresses." For the time being, we lie on the rock beds of the public beach on our pitifully skinny towels. We discuss it when we window shop on the Avenue Jean Medecin and imagine what we will buy. We discuss it when we indulge in beer and socca at our favorite Vieux Nice café and imagine Champagne. I am beginning to address places as "ours" and don't notice when Alec doesn't.

Years later. when I place a large smooth stone in Em's two small outstretched hands and tell her it is sand from Nice, she doesn't believe me and also doesn't include it in her report on beaches and deserts. It is impossible for a seven-year-old child to understand that a stone can also be sand. Before we move to Rockaway, Em's life experience takes place in the middle of Manhattan, where beaches do exist but only on the far reaches of the City's shores and remote as if on another planet.

22

I look for signs of Alec in Em and constantly find them. I am grateful she has his long eyelashes, and a streak of wild animal. Where Alec kept his wide sensuous mouth under a tightly managed script, on Em the same mouth slips and slides and falls where it may; it is generous and free and forgiving and playful.

After a few weeks, Alec tells me his uncle is sending him to Marseilles. The "deal" is coming together. I have mixed feelings. On the one hand, I am happy for Alec that something that has seemed so nefarious yet so important and imminent is really happening. And, thankfully, happening out of town. Though he never says what it was, I know I don't want anything to do with it and also realize I am not invited to. And if we try to mix the deal and our affair up together, both the deal and the affair will fail. Though I can't tell which has more at stake for him, I suspect I can easily be sacrificed. I am also nervous because if it is really happening, I instinctively know everything will be different.

Alec tells me he will be away for a couple of weeks and that he has to "take care of things" in Marseille. Ten days later, I receive a post card from him. The postcard is mailed from Tunisia. I miss him like mad.

"Hot. Really hot. Very dry. That's just the weather. Everything else is OK. A."

Somehow, receiving a post card from Tunisia makes

Alec's story either more, or less, convincing. As I am to learn, Alec's stories are always like that. Uncertain. More or less convincing. More or less. I think sometimes he lies only to see if he can get away with it. But I don't care, as long as he tells me all I want to hear. He is good at that.

He returns to Nice with a small plastic film canister filled with sand, which he pours into the palm of my hand. "Tunis. Here in the palm of your hand." He pours it into my palm. It is warm. As if each grain carries its own small suitcase full of hot Tunisian sun. When Em prepares her report on deserts and beaches, I pour the Tunis sand into her open hand. But by then the little suitcases are abandoned and the grains of sand are cold. Em does include the Tunisian sand in her report.

Everything is different after that. In just the way I realize I've been afraid of.

Alec returns to Nice in a white linen suit, his white cotton shirt now closed shut with a black tie. He is just as pretty, just as handsome. And he basks in his own glory. But somehow, not as young and far from naive, Alec is overnight older. He returns with an age that is like a war medal -- a few years added to his already ambitious ambiguous youth so that it is harder than ever to tell whether he is a mature youngster or looks very young and enticing for his older age. It is as if in those few weeks he's shed a childish cape, a costume that made him magical, in a way masquerading as a youth.

Either way, I am still addictively in love with him. Though growing ever slightly more fretful about our innocent affair.

From then on, Alec insists that we all meet him nightly at the long mahogany bar at the Negresco Hotel. There, Alec orders Veuve Clicquot and expensive sherry. A fat red cat lounges in a chair every night waiting for an elegantly over dressed woman, whom I nickname "la Grande Dame." She lives upstairs and every evening brings the cat a can of expensively prepared cat food. Each evening she presents the open can to the cat and then ritually leaves it with the waiter to serve. Alec reminds me of a slender, black-haired version of the fat red cat who secretly wishes a grande and rich madame would take care of him for the rest of his life. No more sodas. Alec befriends the fat cat in the lounge, the waiters and bartenders, and la Grande Dame. She leaves a faint lingering perfume in the air after flouncing through with her cat food and her demeanor. Occasionally Alec's suit smells faintly of the same perfume.

"After the deal," we do rent chaises and mattresses: Wiley and Marguerite, Jack and Michelle, Alec and me. Marguerite is petite, dark, and exotic; her features all seem to be in miniature, and inside her tiny frame she contains a steely eroticism. I can't fathom what Marguerite sees in Wiley. His skinny concave chest heaves in and out when he is telling a bravura story and his hands weave about in the air; his real name is Riley and I wonder if his nickname is really the result of a Chinaman's jokey description of his wiry body. I suspect that Alec has slept with Marguerite; she is curiously comfortable with him in a way that only people who have been intimate are, and while I am jealously irked each time she saddles up along Alec and he leans his head down toward her, Wiley is indifferent. It is strange being part of a couple, a role neither Alec nor I ever felt comfortable with before, and still don't. For me Alec is a fabulous prize, a trophy to my womanhood, a public relations gesture that advertises my attractiveness. Alec needs no such advertisement; I am instead his shield against his own aloneness. A hedge bet.

And now, Emily. I see Alec in her. I understand my daughter's curiosity about her father, but at some point it begins to feel like an obsession. As if my daughter is a voyeur in the life I shared with Alec, her father, and her curiosity begins to feel intrusive.

"Were there other men?" Emily probes.

"No, not really."

Well, there was that one night with Wiley. I almost forgot it, or, I should say I have forgotten it most of the time and every few years (why?) I remember it. It was just one of those circumstances. Wiley and I are left alone together, waiting, though only casually it seems, certainly not waiting with excitement. It is a hot night, and we fan each other with newspapers. We are waiting the way two people do when they know they are a part of a couple and they are waiting for their "other half." We are glad to have an hour or two with each other's company. Waiting without anxiety, it is sometimes almost a relief, knowing Alec is coming but he is not here yet. And it is much more pleasant when the wait is accompanied by an amusing companion instead of alone.

Wiley is a funny companion; I discover why Marguerite bothers with him at all. He is clever, much more clever than I'd imagined, and much funnier than Alec. Wiley has a sense of humor, a characteristic Alec lost in the make-up of his DNA. Wiley's cleverness makes me laugh out loud, even helps me appreciate Marguerite. His cleverness, and knowing that Alec won't return for a while, turns into a sexual episode that is at once seductive and repulsive. Why do we succumb to these moments?

It's not that I regret those few moments of sweaty sexual intertwining with Wiley, it's only that I don't understand them, and that they have left me with mixed feelings. When I was a girl, I wanted to believe that sex (read love) takes place in pure, perfect moments and that these should be the purest most perfect moments of communion in our lives, uncomplicated by other relationships. But sex is the very act that is more shaped and shared with every other person we have ever loved or trusted. What an illusion to think that sex is the intimate act of two people alone. And to believe it is an act of romance is, well, quixotic.

EPISODE FOUR

Jante and Alec Still

A lec lies gracefully alongside me, comfortable in his chaise, and is clearly pleased with himself, providing his small group of intimate friends with one of life's little luxuries, while the handsome cabana boys serve us all "glacée con framboise" dressed with Liliputian pink and yellow paper umbrellas, and the turquoise lip of Mediterranean laps across the stone beach like the edge of a dull knife.

"I'm going to Marseille with you."

Alec gives me a cold, brief stare.

"You're sure you want to go to Marseille?" Alec

implores me with his bittersweet eyes, which dart away from me. "It's a rough city. Not like the Riviera."

When I am not totally beguiled, it occurs to me that Alec is just practicing on me. Roles that have gotten good reviews before and that he hopes will get better and more lucrative reviews after me. For years I have wondered if they did. I think after all the world really isn't ready for Alec and his kind; a world where la Grande Dame at the Negresco can be completely free to feed him, nurture him. And all his small, practiced expressions and nuances are not wasted but instead earn him an honest living, and even a pension. I am growing by inches more cynical, more afraid of losing him. I'd go anywhere to keep him, and pay any price. The thought of leaving him alone in Marseille terrifies me. I know I'll lose him. Alec is also afraid of confrontation and doesn't tell me outright he doesn't want me to go with him. Instead, he will torture me a little everyday with small rejections. Marseille is really where my innocent resolve about Alec is going to dissolve. It is where we eventually part.

I convince my editor that Marseille is under appreciated as far as the travel market goes and I follow Alec there. I rent an efficiency apartment in Marseille, even though I know Alec prefers a hotel room. It has a large kitchen with an old defunct dumb waiter shaft, a stove in one corner, a sink which we quickly fill with unwashed dishes in another, and a huge open space in the middle which he promises me he will soon fill with a large antique table and flowers in vases. I've learned not to put much faith in Alec's promises; they usually go unfulfilled. Aside from the kitchen, we also have a good size living room where we sleep, watch television, and listen to music. We are making love less and less, though I tell myself it is because he is distracted.

In Marseille I meet the famous deal-making Uncle Eduardo. I'm not sure what to expect, though I am curiously and not unpleasantly surprised to find a short, calloused- looking man who indeed does look more like a French ditch digger than a suave Latin wheeler-dealer and lover. I gradually understand why a woman like Alec's late mother would fall in love with him; he conveys a casual, courteous charm that is disarming and appealing, and though not obviously a womanizer, he clearly likes women. Even me.

Years later, when Em and I are living in the Rockaways, Uncle Eduardo looks me up and calls to say he is in town and can he meet me for a drink after work. We meet at a bar in midtown, and when I shake his hand the skin is still tough and his grip warm and

31

large. He kisses each cheek, French style. I think he might be curious about Em, perhaps recognizing that Em might be his own grandchild, but he doesn't ask about her and I don't speak of her either. Maybe my vaulted secret is well kept, after all.

I've never understood why Eduardo called me during this visit; perhaps it was just curiosity or that small, lingering guilt we all harbor after not seeing old acquaintances for a very long time. I am reminded by this little rendezvous how people who play a prominent role in our lives -- even for a very brief time -- continue to shape and form our thoughts and memories for years and then just disappear as if the world is really flat and they fell off the horizon. I don't hear from him again until Em is in college and he writes to tell us that Alec is gravely ill.

Financially, things are turning toward the worse in Marseilles. Uncle Eduardo has, at least temporarily, abandoned his deal-making and returned to Barcelona. That leaves Alec without a bankroll and to work odd jobs again, tending bar, waiting tables, and more dependent on me. He has no problem getting the jobs and does well with tips, but he hates waiting on others and it leaves him sullen, and after a few drinks, surly. He is spending more time away from me, and being rude and resentful when I ask him where he is going.

It's funny how an innocent question like "Where are you going" has a different meaning when you are hiding something. When you are innocent, "Where are you going" connotes "I want to be with you, I am concerned that you may be someplace where you might be hurt, I care about what you do and what you are interested in, I can't wait until you return." When you are hiding, it means "I don't trust you, you are a liar, you are stealing little bits of my life, I hate you and you must hate me too." On the surface, things appear normal. Though we are both working hard at the appearance, little by little Alec is distancing himself from me. He is drinking copiously and staying away even more. I blame myself and believe I can't do anything right. I try to engage him in discussion but he gets angry. "Can't you see I don't want to talk about this right now?" When then? What about me? What about us?

It is a sad moment when you realize your lover is no longer attending to you. I have heard this from friends whose love affairs and marriages last for three years, seven years, ten and even twenty years. With Alec, the moment came in just more than a year -- it doesn't really matter when. I have to admit to my own complacency but then that intimate disregard happens when your lover avoids your body in the dark, in the middle of the night, and pretend they are asleep, and when you realize it you are crushed. *What about me? What about us?* You want to scream. But you don't. You avoid thinking about it until it is convenient to do so, like when the sun is shining and feelings can be brought out on the table and examined, sorted out, and put away again in the right order.

I despise women who cling to a man, yet I cling to Alec, my tendrils glued to his bark as steadfastly as any vine. But as Alec gradually strips his rough outer layer and sands it to that smooth satin finish it gives me no grip hold; maybe that's why he shed it. I also had to admit the unromantic reality that Alec is my aunt, the same self- distancing aunt who also stood like a venerable old tree in my life, providing a reliable source of shade and fruit but who had no arms to reach out to hug a small girl. I have yet to reconcile the Alec who was steady, my steady, with Alec who roamed not like a tree but more the flower borne by the tree, on top of a breeze that only he could feel, landing wherever the wind took him. We are both terribly unhappy.

"Where are you going?" I ask Alec.

"Going? What do you mean? Where am I going. I'm going to work, where do you think I'm going?"

"Where did you go yesterday? I mean where did you really go yesterday?" I hate myself in this role, the prying, distrustful wife to the philandering husband. I

34

open the mail one day, his mail. It contains a photo of an older woman, an attractive woman, vaguely familiar; where did I know her from? She is wearing a negligee and holding one of her large breasts in her hand, as if it were a jug offering its voluptuous liquid to any thirsty taker -- to Alec.

The envelope also contains a post card, from the Negresco. Ah. Of course. La Grande Dame. "I miss our moments together. Please call me the moment you return." But no, she isn't the one. She is too far away. Too old. Not really old, she is in fact attractive, for a woman her age, but too old for a man like Alec to get distracted over, and again she is too far away. Another postcard from her. "The flame in my blood awaits you, your touch..." Although the post cards help to explain his absences in Nice, and especially the perfume on his jacket, they do not explain the absences in Marseilles.

I am like a spy in my own life now, seeking clues, seeking the truth, looking for pieces of paper, receipts, telephone numbers, dates, anything -- anything that will reveal the truth to me, and when I find it, it nearly breaks me. There is the revelation. It is a letter, this time in Alec's own handwriting, elegant and jolted, expressing romantic and hopeful expressions of love and intimacy that I have longed to hear from him since the first time we'd made love. But the letter isn't addressed to me. He is in love with someone else? I leave the letter on the kitchen counter. "I'm sorry. I read your mail."

Being handed the truth is like a tablet from heaven, like facing God. Enthralling and terrifying, like a storm- swollen ocean that destroys yet cleanses the earth, a cathartic sweeping away and scattering of the dross of old personal myths and attachments. Alec, unfettered by any doubts or regrets about his actions has turned me into the enemy, into a stranger."

"I don't want to send you mixed messages," he announces. "I want to be very clear. There isn't a future for us."

Mixed messages? You've sent only mixed messages since we've met.

EPISODE FIVE

Jante and Emily

My despairing mind tries to grasp that Alec has cut my mooring free and I am a loose vessel, adrift. I simultaneously want to throw myself a life vest and drown. Even though he can be wildly vacillating, and frequently evasive, I was always sure of Alec's affection and his presence.

Now I am both trapped and abandoned, eddying in a dangerous, swirling pool of questions: *when did this begin, what were the warnings?* How determinedly I ignored the switches turning off, the blockades, the small then tiny porthole into his heart closing to a pinhole.

I am also missing my period. It is a strange time for me.

It's not that Alec is a deliberate liar (unless he is practicing), he simply disassembles the truth. He breaks it into packets of information, none of which contain the complete story, and gives each person in his life a different set of packets. Everyone has an idea of what is going on with him, but no one knows everything. To most people in his life, he is very much in the moment, but I know his secret; he lives only in small envelopes of the here and now, doled out like little care packages or like mail to prisoners of war. I wonder how he keeps track of which packet went to whom, and if he ever put all the packets together, would they present the whole picture? Does Alec himself ever see the complete picture? I doubt he does. There are too many gray gaps between what he sees, experiences, feels, and says, as if he lives in a discontinuous world, like an unfinished jigsaw puzzle. So of all his little packets of truth I am now being allowed only one: Get out. Black and white. No more grays.

My aunt who raised me, too, loved me from a safe distance; so I don't have an adequate ruler with which to measure emotional constancy. Perhaps it isn't odd that I would choose someone like Alec to depend on.

And I know I am one to him too; like a barometer, I am the one he uses to gauge the weather of his feelings. Am I stormy or calm today? Except now he forgets his lines, or has them mixed up, and he is breaking the dramatic rules. Now he only hides from me, his weather, and plays the part of the cheating husband according to script.

Alec and I live similarly unfinished, incomplete, undone lives. Fragments of the past and little hints of the future. Is there a future? I pretend to plan for it, I cherish it -- at least as a remote idea. But I too live as if there is no tomorrow. Here and now. This minute. And in this minute, everything that matters is already happening. And when the moment is over, whatever happened in it is burned up. Like a comet. Dazzling. Then dead.

I want him to tell me about the lies he'd written to her, all lies. *"Take them back! Those words are meant for me!"* *"Of course. I'm so sorry; please forgive me. I really love you. She doesn't mean anything to me."*

"No. I'm not going to take them back."

"But I'm your lover." *What about me? What about us?*

"No. No. Not anymore. I'm not in love with you, Jante. Janet. I've never been in love with you. I love you, but I'm not in love. I'm sorry."

Now every act between Alec and me, even an act as natural as sleeping together, feels absurdly unnatural, as if he is a giraffe and I am a deer, odd bedfellows instead of lovers. We are in fact like road kill and starting to smell bad. Infidelity is a strange animal that throws your loyalty into the camp of a complete stranger and turns your best friend into the enemy. I am the enemy. Careening through a whitewater river of emotions set loose by Alec's confession, I call my editor, say I am ill. My voice is raw and he questions me.

"You sound terrible," he says. "Is everything all right?"

"No. No. I am ill." Ill with rage and fear and ravaging pain.

Meanwhile, the little seed has been planted. Every morning I pray not to see blood. I want that little seed. It gives me a root hold on life that I need, even more than I need Alec. To replace Alec. I take the train to Nice to meet privately with my editor and explain what is happening, why I must leave. I do not tell Alec about the seed and make my plan to return to the States with it secreted away in my belly. Now my love for Alec has to be spent quickly, like a gambler throwing it all away in one last gasping bet on the number Two. A pair of hearts.

The weeks spent packing and waiting for my flight to New York are tense and torturous. As if Alec and I are scaling a shifting mountain. I sort through my clothes, books, dishes, art, collections of odds and -- at the time I acquired them --wonderful ends. Each item goes into one of three piles: leave, take, discard. It is like undoing a puzzle that I'd spent the last five years in France composing and assembling. First, the sky. Then, the house. Next, the trees and flowers. One article at a time, my life is being taken apart.

I work, too, at dismantling the larger-than-life image I have created of Alec. First, his aura of mystery, his Wizard of Oz gimmickry. Now that I have peeked behind the curtain, I am tempted to tear it aside and reveal his naked manipulation to everyone. Especially to Alec. Aha! I've caught you. I harbor a secret, perverse joy, imagining Alec scrambling to pull the cords and strings that make his charade possible. But I leave him alone. Why destroy the man? Second, his supplication of women. Another disguise. Once off your pedestal, he can more easily trample you. Third? I'm not sure. His sexuality? I was never sure if he preferred men over women; he doesn't seem to care about a person's sex as long as it is available.

I struggle with the shells and stones I'd collected over the years on the Mediterranean, especially the large smooth pebbles from the beach in Nice. I put them in my bag. I take them out. Finally, I decide to keep the largest one. It is quiet and solid, the way I like to think of Nice, its streets and buildings keeping silent about its past.

Alec's usually closed interior is now locked to me. It is foolish, but I can't help but try every approach, short of a crowbar. Unsuccessfully. The inner man remains as hard and opaque as a marble obelisk. The pin hole closes as if there had never been an opening, like alien fabric.

Meanwhile, I have my own secret. The seed that now will be the size of an acorn. I imagine it as a small, perfect person that I confess to and share my pain with. And as my seed grows larger, it listens. And Alec shrinks. One day Alec will be so small I can hold him in my hand. And then he will become so small, the size of a seed, that I can toss him to the wind. Despite my emotional pain during those weeks, my body moves through them, and somehow, the rest of me follows.

Alec and I treat each other with kindness and with disdain. I know he believes he is being caring of me, but I also know he only wants me to think well of him. And also that he wants me to be gone. In a normal person, my presence would accentuate his guilt at abandoning me, but for Alec, it just reminds him of his desire to be free of me. But the conflict: *think well of me, get out*, is too hard for him to reconcile. And now it is something like a stab wound healing. The worst over. Before the crisis, one person. After the crisis, a different person. A better one. Smarter. Older, certainly older. Perhaps if I'd seek out the real Alec, and tell him, "Don't worry, be yourself. People will still like you." But I am too busy defending myself. And the likelihood that Alec would know that person -- himself -- is unlikely.

EPISODE SIX

Emily and Eduardo

I know my mother has been deeply disappointed for years by the break-up with Alec. He stood in for the family she didn't have. And then I did. But I need a family, too. I am curious about Alec. My mother's answers about him are stilted and colored by her never-to-be-satiated longing for him.

Then one Saturday, as if on cue, we receive a card from Eduardo. It is a simple card, one of those you find in a pack of cheap foreign holiday cards. A smiling bear clutches a cluster of daisies and gaily announces

"Hola! Alexandro ill." And a phone number. Signed, "Eduardo M...."

"Eduardo? My father? What does he mean, ill...?"

The little missive thrills me. The specter of Alec, my father, being ill doesn't register with me yet, but having an uncle whose handwriting I can actually touch, Alexandro written in long hand, a phone number, makes my heart race a little, and then the message "Alexandro ill" makes me feel as if I am in an old movie or a novel where relatives still write each other notes and send telegrams. A movie that features a family, and I am a member of it.

My mother fingers the card and places it on top of her "to-do" pile; she calls it her pile of "good intentions."

"Are you going to call him?"

"We'll see."

I eye the card, and her, and we both pretend to ignore it. My mother and I have lived alone together long enough to know what each other is probably thinking and then avoid discussing it. We are both more comfortable talking about her past than either of us is each other's present.

But she knows my curiosity about Alec, my father, will force her to call Eduardo. I don't ask her how she feels about Alec being "ill," whatever that means, though I am sure she is thinking about it, and about him in a new and fresh way. If I were my mother, I could let the innocent- looking envelope languish on my desk indefinitely until more and more current "good intentions" obscure it and put a safer distance of time between me and it.

Over next Sunday's morning coffee and the *New York Times*, she says, "Maybe *you* should call him."

Later that week when my mother is out, I arm my-self with my high school Spanish and a dictionary. I am nervous when I pick up the receiver. I've never made a call to Europe before.

"Diga."

"Sr Eduardo M…..?"

"Si." This is long and drawn upward at the end, to signal that Eduardo is more curious than suspicious.

"Mi nombre es Emily…. La hija de Jante. En Nueva York. Perdon mi espanol. Ustedes enviaron – una carte a mi madre, de Alexandro."

"Si! Como esta? Como su madre? Do you speak English? Of course you do! You received my card then. Si …Alexandro is very sick. Not well. Tell me, how is your mother? How is New York? What is she doing, is she still a writer? Is she married?"

"Si. Si.Yes, she is doing well. No, she never mar-ried. I, I don't know if she ever told you…" I hesitate.

"Que…?"

"Well," I wait and then I blurt, "Alexandro es mi padre…"

Silence.

"Hello?"

"Que…" This time the single syllable is drawn out and down as if Eduardo slid on the pavement wearing his best suit, afraid of soiling it and embarrassed at his clumsiness.

"Que. Hombre."

After a deep sigh, he continues.

"Es su nombre es Em….?"

"Emily."

"Emeely. Si. Hombre. La hija de Alexandro. No se Alexandro tiene una hija, he never told me."

"He doesn't know. Jante never told him."

"Ahhh. And now Alexandro, he is in hospital, in Paris. He is not alone, his friend is there, Eric, but he should know…. Yes, he should know about you, before… before he sees you… before he…"

Mother shares a photo with me. Eduardo and Esteban. attractive young men, smiling, and leaning against a car with a rumble seat gaping open, looking as if they'd just waxed it together. One is shorter than the other, with a jocular boyish grin and soft shoulders. The other is taller, thinner, more angular and his smile is more circumspect, more secretive. She said, "Alec would ask me, 'Which one do you think is my father?' I've seen him view it through a magnifying glass and then look at himself in the mirror, checking for similarities between their arms, their gestures, their expressions, and he'd ask me to even compare the little crinkles in the corner of their eyes."

EPISODE SEVEN

Giselle and Esteban and Eduardo

When Eduardo hangs up, he is both smitten and mortified.

Hombre. This reminds me. Too much! Of another surprise. Of Alexandro. I'll never forget that day. The phone call to Giselle, there I was, running away, as fast as I could, by train to Marseille, Genoa, Madrid, it didn't matter. It was Madrid, I think. I just had to get as far away from Giselle, from mad Giselle and wonderful sane Esteban, from them, no, from me, from me and Giselle, as far, as fast as I could. I can never describe that moment when I reached her and she told me. Heartbreak! Oh God, yes, my heart breaks in that moment of news, for my brother, for Giselle, for all of us. And yet, in that same moment, gleeful! Exuberant! Crazy. I do not know what to do, to think; what can I do? Especially, running away. As I should have! As far, far away and as fast as possible! Sooner.

I'd already been hanging around their apartment too long, too many nights, and way, way too many days. The days were far more dangerous than the nights. The nights were agitating, but easy. With Esteban at home after work, everything took on a safe feeling. As long as Esteban was there, we were all safe. And when my agitation obsessed me, I'd leave; there were plenty of women for me. I had no trouble with women, except there were sometimes too many. And they all want something they can't have. Not with me, at least. Why are women like that? They want that very thing you can't give them. And they can't even explain what it is. Oh, yes, they want that thing between your legs, but something else that doesn't come attached to it or come out of it. Attachment, that's it. I can't give them that. And the less I give it the more they want it. So on many nights I just go to the whores.

"Going out?"

"How much?"

"Ten and ten." Ten for the girl and ten for the room.

Only when Esteban left, in the morning, for work. And me, the ugly brother! The no-good brother. Alone in that tiny apartment, inside those four walls, alone with Giselle.

The first time I saw Giselle, I knew we had trouble! My brother brought her home.

"Eduardo. Meet my new wife! Giselle. She's beautiful. Isn't she beautiful?"

Giselle. My brother's wife. Yes, she is beautiful! Just my lucky day, she is the prettiest woman I have ever seen! Strawberry-blonde hair that comes unbound, everywhere, even though she wears a hat, a hat that tips over and makes her look as if she is about to lose her balance, until I finally realize it is not the hat or her hair but her eyes that seem to pitch her off balance. Or is it me? Off balance. No, it is her eyes. One brown. One blue. Not me.

Her giddy glee at everything she sees in the glum living room fills it as if with a thousand small trilling birds! I find myself looking between the brown eye and the blue. Back and forth between them. Like between two women locked, or folded, into the same face, the same hairdo and dress. Is it me? Caught between the mirror images of two sisters, or twins?

Is it the eyes?
Or is it the "Yes" in her eyes?

It is Franco days and everything is in a state of perpetual repression and darkness. Intellectual poverty: thought, desire, money. All static on the surface, brimming just below. My brother Esteban, the good Esteban, works as a teacher and for extra money helping the neighbor in his bicycle shop. I look for "opportunities." Sometimes I am lucky and find one. He provides the basics. I hustle for the extras, what we call "life's little luxuries." My brother is the breadwinner and continues to share the apartment with me. Except now so does my brother's wife.

That first night. The wedding night! I listen to them making love. Her high pitched sharp little "ohs" sound like a child pretending to be stabbed. I masturbate. A million Eduardos puddle in my hand at her last pointed "oh."

For the next eight months I sleep with the other women. The ones who want what I can't give. Sleeping away from the close, dark apartment. As often as possible I avoid my brother and his wife. I rely on my business deals in Madrid and abroad. They give me a safe distance. In the beds of other women, I close my eyes. I seek the smell in their hair and skin as only Giselle smells when she steps from her morning shower. If the woman I am sleeping with has blue eyes? I'll close one eye and just look into it and think of Giselle's blue eye. And if she has brown eyes? Well, the same.

After a few successful deals, I have enough money to leave the little apartment with its grim entrance and its thousand trilling birds inside. But I keep coming back. Giselle's small sharp "ohs" haunt me and strike me through like a needle and a thread. I think of myself as her button. And she is my buttonhole.

One morning, Giselle is pressing a shirt for me. Its starchy whiteness feels special to me. I roll up the crisp sleeves toward my elbows and button the front toward my throat. The few sparrows who live in our barren courtyard trill, outdoors this time. The twenty-five minutes of mid-morning sun that blesses the narrow window over the sink trickles in. Giselle, with just the faintest remains of her morning shower fragrance, offers, "Coffee, Eduardo?"

Giselle's silky arm holds out the china pot. This is the last remaining piece of Mama's wedding set. The rest of it was shattered or fractured by forty-six years of the tumult known as our Papa. His meanness was wrapped inside deliberate, stingy acts of kindness meant for recognition: "See, I'm nice to you. Isn't that nice of me...?" But even the kindest acts, and the generosity, were warped by this meanness. Like a bitter seed inside sweet fruit. After a period of time, he stopped the pretense of the kind acts. Then his "niceness" was revealed for what it really was -- an armor and defense against facing his own meanness, his own smallness.

Mama, God help her, never became angry. Oh no, no, that's wrong. She never showed anger. No. She receded, like a clam inside a shell. Or an ebbing tide. Just going away, a little at a time. You couldn't reach her then. She would become quiet. Like she would just disappear, or like she wanted to. Then he would stop noticing her. And he would find us. Me. Especially, me. The "bandido." Happy to talk back and willing to make trouble, to distract him from her, from my brother. He'd grab me by the ear. And then start. Oh, my ears still hurt from his grabbing! And Esteban, poor brave Esteban! Standing up for all of us. Our shield.

When Papa had too much to drink, I couldn't stand him. I never saw him "drink too much" or drinking at all. Not in excess. He drank alone. And then he became a very ugly person. Then he acted on a dishonestly cheerful skin-deep level like a bad New Year's Eve when everyone fakes frivolity and lightness, masking chaos and loneliness.

When he was drunk, we would notice the change, instinctively, and would take up our defensive positions.

Mama in the kitchen. Esteban doing his homework. And me, the decoy, planning the mischief. In the beginning, their fights led to rowdy lovemaking in my parents' bedroom. I covered my ears not to hear them.

With feelings, Papa was more the blunt instrument than the surgeon, though he understood anger. It was the only feeling he expressed clearly, where he was articulate. Maybe that's why he used it most. To express all feelings. Even love. Oh, and then remorse. That was the other feeling he knew well. It's true. We are all awful company when we've had too much to drink. And the remorse afterwards doesn't make us better people. Just remorseful drunks. "Whatdya think?" he'd ask, drunk and not really looking for an answer. Just making drunk noises. "Think? About what? What. What? What?" What do I think about drunks? I think your lies and and your remorse make me doubt my own sanity.

Many times, instead of sounds from the bedroom, I could hear Mama crying. She would run the water into the bathtub and who knows? Probably sitting on the toilet. Crying her pretty eyes out. Maybe thinking about taking Papa's razor and cutting her wrists. Or his throat.

Only once did Mama show her anger. It was the only time he stopped. I don't know what life was like for her before Esteban and me. This one time, though, she shouted at him, "You pig! You shit-faced pig! I hate you!"

She threw a plate of his food at him. No, that's wrong. After she stopped shouting, she served him his plate. She didn't throw it. She dropped it in his lap. And of course it didn't stay in his lap, it fell to the floor. The ham. The rice. The garbanzos. The china. All falling in slow motion. Meat! China! Rice! All crackling against the cold blue tile floor. Jumping up again toward all of our astonished faces! Except Mama's face. She was the only one of us not surprised. Esteban and I both stopped chewing. Stunned! We stopped and held our breath. Papa became quiet. I'd never seen him so quiet. He even helped her pick up the broken pieces. I'm pretty sure it was the only piece of their china she ever broke. Her cherished wedding set. And the food. He loved her cooking. He sat down at the table, and she served him another plate. I swear he looked at the food on his plate as if the food might eat him instead. I almost wanted to laugh! If I hadn't been so terrified, I might have laughed. And then they acted as if nothing happened. We all ate in silence, my stomach aching in a tight, small ball! I didn't eat much that night. Esteban and I are pretty sure that one night, maybe that night, she turned her back to him in bed and never turned around again.

"Coffee, Eduardo?"

Giselle's delicate hands look naked to me, except for the thin gold band placed there -- precariously, I think -- by my brother, in a fit of extravagance otherwise unknown to him in his placid life. My brother, blessedly? I wonder, works regular hours and depends upon his routine to keep order in his life, and to keep his own anarchy at bay. Unlike the wayward, unshaven, and happy-go-lucky -- sometimes lucky -- usually down on his luck brother, Eduardo.

"Coffee, Eduardo?" As she brews the steamy, strong- smelling coffee into Mama's last teapot, I read to her from the morning paper, a story about a man and his dog, wedding announcements, a poem. I read to her, from Gabrielle D'Annunzio.

"Breathe it in, Francesca. The scent does you good. He said these simple words in an understated tone of voice, as he would have spoken the vehement beginning of a love lyric. The festival of his youth burst out luminously, he did not repress it, he did not wish to repress it. No kind of happiness is sweeter than being at the loved one's side..." I skip the part about the horseback ride, "...those upsurgings of barbaric freedom, which men have in their blood, made him now forget his brother." I do not read "His brother's wife was beautiful and he was winning her." I keep that to myself.

The thin ring dangles indifferently on her naked left hand. It looks large and alien, like a life raft on an old rickety boat, or out at sea. How her hands appeared naked to me I do not understand. My own hands do not. I glance at them to make sure. No. They are clothed; although the skin is exposed, I may as well be wearing thick leather gloves.

Her neck, too, appears naked. Shamelessly naked. I want to wrap a large soft shawl around her throat to protect it from predators. From me.

I carefully, purposefully touch her naked, vulnerable hand with my clothed one as I hold my teacup out for her.

Giselle's eyes pierce mine and for once I see them both together. The brown and the blue. For once, Giselle is one woman, whole and complete. I am no longer off balance as I take her into my arms and kiss her, aching for one small sharp "oh," clinging to her eyes. We make love that way. From now on we make love that way. Three brown eyes and one blue. Holding on fast to each other like life jackets to keep from drowning. To keep me from falling overboard.

Instead of the small sharp "ohs," though, a thick, guttural sound that frightens and thrills me seems to growl out of the pores of her skin. Her mouth hangs open, spilling over with those sounds. Like water over stones, like an open wound, a possessed thing awaiting a tongue, a mouth, a soul. My soul. To silence its ungodliness.

I leave a note in the pocket of her bathrobe, the one that smells of her after a shower.

"Mi fuego dulce." Sweet fire. That is what I call her now. "I know it is not possible to extract such pleasure from another human being without taking some responsibility for them. I have a little money this month. Can I buy you something? A new dress? Pretty shoes? Be careful, though, my brother will suspect where it came from." I find a note in my pocket that night. And after many more nights, more notes:

Eduardo, Mi amor:

You are so able to handle my emotions. I awake feeling full, alive, well. I used to wake up and find myself like an old dress with seams tattered and spread apart and now my seams are ironed over like new cloth. Thank you, Eduardo.

P.S. I saw a pretty red dress and matching shoes at the Emporio that I would like very much. They are in the window. G

Eduardo, Mi amor:

My emotions are at home with you. You are an artist and you are not afraid of my palette of colors and I am just paint to your brush. G.

Eduardo, Mi amor:

I think you should bottle me and sell me as a euphoric to all the unfortunates who do not have you to fill them with joy. G.

Mi amor:

You garden me as if I am a wild vine, you contain me and direct my growth to become something beautiful, free and yet commanded. G.

Mi amor:

I love you, Eduardo. I love your flesh, your essence, the smell of your hair and the sounds that came out of you. I love my husband too, I could not survive without him, he is so kind, so firm, I would fly apart without him. G.

Eduardo...

You know mi passuardi, my passion, you know everything about me. And you don't care about any of those things. About any of that! Your brother... now, he cares, he is wonderful, about all of that. But you don't care about anything, about me. You just go about your life and assume that I will still be there, just like the moments you leave me, the moments I am at my weakest, you know those moments, they are all the moments you leave me. Totally weak. Not spent. Weak. You know how difficult it is for me to do what I want to do for you, I want to be the one who is always there for you. The constant one. The one who is like the favorite old chair with a cup of tea and rum and warm socks and a fire burning. That's who I want to be. But you know me, too. I am not those things, instead I need those things myself, the fireplace, the logs, just the right tea, the socks and warm feet. You are too much like me and not only can I not depend on you for these things, I know that one day some pretty girl will come along and claim them from you and take you away from me at the same time that I am terrified of losing you I will also be relieved. Meanwhile I know I cannot depend on you and therefore also hope, wish that you will leave me alone, just leave me alone. G.

I find this latest missive from Giselle in my jacket pocket on the train heading toward Madrid. Running away again, away from the trilling birds and cockeyed eyes. I can see her, in my mind's eye, stomping around the little apartment, the thousand trilling birds suddenly transformed into a troop of gypsy flamenco dancers!

And my poor brother not knowing what was wrong or what to do about it. He would set the logs and stoke a cozy fire. He would try to calm her with soft words and a blanket, and she would push him away.

I am glad I am not there. It makes it easy for me to "leave her alone"! I think, angrily, that I should, would, leave her alone! But parallel to that thought is my memory of her. Her face placed into the crook between my throat and my shoulder blade. Her morning shower smell tainted with the horny smell of her sex. And my hand on her breast. Like a gentle captivator's hand around a timid swallow.

Leave her alone. I would like to! Would I? Could I? Beside me, not just me, Giselle lacked the will, the discipline to stay away, to leave *me* alone...

The last time I sat with her she said, "Things are easier for me and Esteban when you go away. Things settle down. We live like beautiful old married people."

She paused and looked out over the table where we sat, past me, past the apartment. Into a place I've never been to and would probably never visit.

"It's comfortable."

"Like an old chair?" I chided her.

"Yes. Yes. Like a safe, old chair. I love that old chair. I want to just get into that beautiful old chair and sleep there, or just escape everything there..."

But I know Giselle! I know the part of her that loves danger. And loves me because I don't live safely. Like my brother does. The old chair. She likes life's raw serrated edges, and in fact, she is one herself. And her raw edge cuts into me. Right into my stomach! I feel as if I have swallowed a sword. Leave her alone? It would be best to end it fast, like a razor cut.

I call Giselle from the next station. I hear her breathing, measured and uncertain, as if she is laboring under a large stone.

"Giselle?" I pause, and she continues to breathe, heavily. "Are you all right?"

"Yes. No. I don't know. Eduardo?"

"Yes?"

"I need you to touch me." She breathes again, hard, fast, and shallow. "Eduardo?"

"Yes, Giselle?"

"I think, I... think. Eduardo, I am pregnant."

Pregnant?

Mine?

My brother's?

Really, darling? What does one say? That's wonderful? This is terrible? I feel both ways and say nothing.

"Eduardo?"

"Yes," I sigh, deeply, and resigned, "I'm here."

"Did you hear what I said?"

The train whistle blows.

"Yes."

Yes. I am off balance again, tipping overboard.

"Giselle. Listen. I'm sorry. I have to go! I have to get back on the train. I'm sorry... listen... I'm sorry... yo querro... I ... I'm sorry... I've got to get this train... again... hello??.. I'll call you later..." I hear one of her small "ohs" echo into the receiver as I hang up and run back to the train, just making it. Just making it! Always, just making it.

My brother, however, makes it. He entwines his sinuous, safe, life-saver body around Giselle's, every night. I, instead, am lost at sea, desperately seeking Esteban, too, as my life saver, my life jacket, you my brother who served as my surrogate, my twin, my other half, taking the gaffe, protecting me with your placid solid wall of cold war defense against our parents, and me, the wild one, distracting them with my mayhem. I don't know who I want to sleep with more, Giselle or my brother. One for passion. One for safety.

I do call later, much later -- days, actually. I am distracted, distraught. I wonder how my brother stands it. The soft impetuous, secret (we believe!) brush of hand against hand. The stupidly, impetuous moments whispering "I love you." "Yo quiero, please touch me," and all the while it is my brother who makes the secure nest possible. He pays the rent. He pays the electric. He pays the phone even when I call collect to speak to his darling wife.

Does he love Giselle so much? He can't not notice that she wants me, that she is with me, any moment, every moment we can respond to our mutual self-destruction, our shared obsession.

Or does he love me that much? Enough to pretend to ignore us, to act as if everything really is as normal as it appears. And for him, it is; that is his secret way of managing life. I have never had a steady job, no way of "making a living," whatever that is. Instead I make money here (big) and there (little) and yet he accepts this arrangement. He is the one who makes sure there is a roof (always) and electricity (always) I am the one to make sure there will be steaks (occasionally), radios and then televisions (occasionally), and now even pretty red dresses.

This is our joint style, how we have always lived together. And now so does Giselle. She looks to him for the roof, the comfortable slippers. I bring the champagne and the matching red shoes.

No wonder we make her mad! Poor Giselle.

And now? What? My poor brother. I love him so much; in a way this is our child. We're finally going to be able to raise the boy we both wanted to be, to become, and couldn't partly because we had to compete with each other, but even more so because we had to join forces, fighting for our parents' attention to keep us alive, and to do less than that meant we'd both be dead. I wonder how my mother survived. In the early days, after a fight they'd make up in boisterous love-making. Once Papa had decided he no longer needed the cloak of kindness, his bitterness and fear became a barbed poisoned arrow that left my mother sullen and wounded. He'd tiptoe around her for a few days until the bruises healed, and then he'd get confident again, then pushy again, then mean again.

I am surprised to hear my brother's voice on the other end of the line,. I expected he'd have left for work by now.

"Did you hear? Giselle. Giselle. Oh God, She's beautiful. You know she's beautiful! But now! She's pregnant too. My beautiful Giselle. Pregnant, having a baby!"

"Are you sure?"

I realize immediately this is a stupid, wrong response. My brother, who is genuinely (I think!) happy does not hear, or pretends not to hear, my distress, anyone's distress. Aside, he says to me, "Eduardo, speak to her, please talk to her. Her eyes are as red as wine; I can tell she has been crying. She is frightened, poor thing; you know how she is, afraid of everything -- talk to her, you can always bring her to a smile. Anyway, she is having a baby. A baby! Eduardo. My life will be complete. You, Giselle, and now... what do you think, Eduardo, a boy? Just like you and me. A girl? Like Giselle. I don't care. A little French girl like her mother, pretty and smart and French. Not like us."

"Yes? Yes, that is wonderful, wonderful news..." This time I get it right, the right modulation, the right enthusiasm. I love my brother so much; I want desperately to believe it is his son, his daughter. With all my heart I want it to be his!

If I could have read my brother's mind (and sometimes I think I do) here is what he would have said:

"Many people would wonder. How can I stand to have my wife, my beautiful precious wife, and my brother, my tenderest love, embrace? I cannot explain, except to say this. I love them each as if they are my own flesh. I love them each as if we are all one person, divided for now, but really not separate. Take Giselle. I knew the moment I set my eyes on her even from a distance, I saw her coming at me. I saw her maneuvering toward me. As if she were the spring and I was an old dried-up garden, I saw her approach and I began to be enlivened by her promise, and her presence just engulfed me. Pretend for example that you are standing on a train platform. That is not exactly how I met Giselle, but as a model of what it was like, it will do. So. There you are. On the platform. Where are you going? It doesn't matter. That's part of the problem and also by the way part of the charm when she does come along. Because suddenly, here is Giselle. Where is she going? Well, what a surprise; that's where I want to go too! So, you see a pretty woman approach you, and also, by the way, you're certain she has a destination separate from yours and what dumb stupid luck when you learn she hasn't, and in fact, what luck! You happened on her path at just the right moment to give her exactly the same direction you yourself are seeking.

"I know. I know. These are not sound foundations for a marriage. But had you been me and it was Giselle approaching, you'd have done the same. I mean marry her, of course. Because after all she may have been the spring to my winter garden, but in fact she was the fragile flower, the bud that wanted for attention and care and the strength and the steady hand of a gardener, and although I wanted to be a flowering bush myself, I would always be a gardener. Despite my desire to be cared for, I was always the strong caretaker. And so, I married her as quickly as possible because I was afraid less of losing her than that she would die if I didn't. And with all my life I want to be her hero."

He was always my hero. Every day. Since the day I was born. There is strong, steady Esteban, looking over me. Absorbing life. Making sure I am all right. And now, Giselle. And soon, a child. All of us all right. Because of him.

I stay away for most of the months when Giselle is bearing her child. I think of it mostly as Giselle's child, as if she had immaculately conceived it. When I am there, Giselle seems oddly aloof during these months, even wistful, and looks past me through the little window over the kitchen sink and pours my coffee absentmindedly, distracted as if she is peering into her own womb, concentrating on compiling the cells, the hair, and the eyes of her offspring. Once, when she is beginning to show, and we are alone, she pulls up her dress. Her pubic hairs form a perfect small triangle of light, soft, brown hair, and her stomach is stretched hard and smooth like a large polished stone under my curious hands, disturbed only by the minute protuberance of the child wrestling inside her, "Baby's first steps," she proclaims. We make love only occasionally until she is nearly due; then it is impossible to deny her pregnancy, and my potential role in it.

EPISODE EIGHT

Eduardo and Giselle

It gets easier for awhile after the baby is born. A boy. Alexandro Eduardo Esteban. My brother and I choose, odds or evens, whose name will go first. "Ah Eduardo, you win, you are always the lucky one." Alexandro distracts all of us from our private grief. Watching him grow becomes a favorite pastime. His first smile, his hair growing in. Sitting up. Do I look for signs of myself in him? All the time. Do I see them? Often. Luckily, he takes on more of his mother's finer looks than either of his "fathers'." He is pretty, like Giselle. Dark hair, chestnut eyes, a sensuous mouth.

A beautiful boy, he attracts attention wherever he goes. Men and women both take to him; he is a little magnet.

But in personality I know he will be like me. I see the mischief in him and encourage it. Where Esteban sees his tenderness, I see the rogue. Where Esteban sees an honest tradesman-to-be, I see a wanderer. Where Esteban sees an artist, I see a trickster, a deal-maker. Just like me. Just like me.

Giselle and I remain lovers, on and off. On and off. The flame doesn't die. It smolders until one of us fans it. And voilà! There I am, between the blue and the brown. Clasping her delicate wrist. I spend fewer nights there but when I do? Out of the corner of my eye I see the gentle hollow behind Giselle's neck. I catch a glimpse of the inside of her arm, where it bends to dress Alexandro in his pajamas. I sleep -- barely, restlessly -- on the couch, waiting for morning. For Esteban to leave for work. And now for Giselle to walk Alexandro to school. And I wait for her return. And when we are alone in the apartment, the trilling begins again and I am lost. Like a schoolboy myself. A truant, though. Breaking the rules, again.

What changes then? Do I finally grow up? Am I sick of myself? Sick with shame? Or do I finally meet another woman who can distract me from Giselle. Make me forget her, for days at a time. It is amazing and free! To wake up after a few days and remember that I'd forgotten to think of Giselle.

It is only a matter of time before Giselle realizes something is different. I have not been there in months. And when we do speak by phone, she asks me, "What is going on?" I hear the frantic nervousness bubbling to the surface. And I assure her "Nothing, Giselle, nothing is 'going on.' Everything is still the same. Except, well, except. We can't make love anymore. We have to, we must stop. This has to stop. Finally."

She hangs up with a small sharp "oh," like the child being stabbed again. And I know I must explain to her. I hope she will be glad. Not frantic. She can finally settle herself down. Into the old chair.

But rather, I get her letter. Not a happy one.

Eduardo,

You say nothing has really changed that really everything is still the same, except for the love making. To you it is a small change. So we will no longer make love and everything else will be the same. Eduardo! What are you thinking of? Everything has changed, nothing is the same! I thought you were my best friend, mi compañero, that you would always be my lover. Now after ten – almost eleven! -- years, you are deserting me. Changing everything. Not one thing. All things! I am miserable losing all these things: my friend, my lover, my conspirator, all at once. I have to hide my tears from Esteban and Alexandro. But I cannot hide my nervousness, I am short with them and I do not want to leave my bed. And who is this woman? I heard Esteban speak of her; he said you are living with her, that you are maybe even in love with her, Eduardo, mi amor, why didn't you tell me yourself? Why do I have to pry these things from you? You know I have never said you shouldn't see other women, how could I do that – oh, I would have liked to, you know how jealous I am, but I could hardly say to you, don't, when I sleep each night in another man's bed. So that man is your brother. You know I would have left Esteban to live with you, but you would never even let me finish that sentence. You just closed yourself up, like a window, slammed shut if I brought up the idea. Yes, just like a window. I could see you through it, I could even see my own reflection in it, but I couldn't reach you, as if the glass were soundproof and all you could do was see my lips moving. But living with her? In love with her? How you desert me, betray me, us. And not even confide in me that you were having these feelings for another woman? It's my fault, isn't it? My moods – I know, I know – these are hard to take, Esteban is so good, so sure, he is my cave in a hurricane, and poor little

Alexandro, he has to take shelter from me, and yet, I must be crazy, I chose you... the wandering brother, to cling to. Last night I left Alexandro and Eduardo, for a little while. I rode the bus to Barceloneta. I went to the water. I took a little flower with me, you know the one, the little plant with the purple flowers on the windowsill over the sink; you and I picked it out at the market. "A passion flower," I said, "Like you," you said. I took off my shoes and stepped into the water. What would it be like to keep going? It was so easy just keep walking deeper and deeper until I was swallowed whole like a raisin by my mother, the sea. But I became afraid of the waves and just pulled one petal – "He loves me," and another, "He loves me not." I learned that from an American boyfriend. He always made sure there were just the right number of petals to end on "He loves me." Last night mine ended on "not" and I tossed the petals, all of them, into the waves and said goodbye to you, to our love.

Eduardo, I wanted to toss myself into the waves too! My heart is breaking, like the waves, crashing and noisy yet somehow still beating in a regular rhythm. But I remembered Alexandro and imagined Alex and Esteban sitting at the table together, maybe playing cards, Esteban serving up cookies and a cup of warm milk for Alex* and I turned away from my mother. "No raisin treat for you tonight, ma mère!' P.S. *He is more like you everyday, perhaps I haven't lost you after all. G-

And then I receive another letter.

Eduardo-

I had another one of those horrible anxiety attacks today, it was unexpected. It was as if it had taken complete control of my brain waves, as if an alien presence had entered through the top of my head and began sucking me out of my body through a hole in my skull. I thought, "Well, I'll just go lose myself in a movie for a couple of hours." Well, I almost did. I took the last empty seat in the house, climbing over five other people to reach it, and before long the alien began sucking me out of myself and I was surrounded by people, just calm people waiting to watch a movie and I felt like the whole house was closing in on me, the movie, the popcorn, the audience, and I had to climb back over the same people, as fast as I could, I had to get out, I don't know where I would have gone had I just sat there, probably mad. G

It is to be the last letter I will ever receive from Giselle.

And now. This new surprise. Alexandro. A father. Imagine! Dio! I might be a grandfather! What is her name? Here it is, Emeely. New York, 212-682-9265.

She must see Alexandro. He must know her before. Well, just before.

She will call Alexandro's friend, Eric. Eric will take care of things. Eric has always taken care of things. Like another Esteban, that Eric. But queer. Well, so what. To each his own. Alexandro was more wild than me! Everyone. He fucked everyone. I will tell Emeely she must call Eric. She must visit Alexandro. Yes, that's an answer.

EPISODE NINE

Emily and Eric

After speaking to Uncle Eduardo, I am worldly. I have a father in hospital (not in THE hospital) in Paris and an Uncle in Barcelona. Who knows what kind of ancestors I have, a Spanish Contessa, a famous Parisian courtesan, pirates. Uncle Eduardo suggests I speak to my father's friend, Eric. Eric Coyne, Interior Designer, Paris.011-33 etc. And now I have a French decorator. I am reborn and this time with my best high-school French I am armed and ready to attack Paris.

I call Eric Coyne.

"Allo?"

"Je m'appelle Emily. Parlez-vous Anglais?"

"Allo. Mais oui. Yes, yes."

"I wonder, if you know, do you know, where Alexandro M-- is ? I am looking for Alexandro M--- , his uncle, Uncle Eduardo, Eduardo suggested I call you…"

Emily? Who is this new threat? He doesn't, he never revealed anything to me, just "Oh Eric, I need some money. I'll suck your cock later."

"Oui, yes, A is here." So to speak, he is here; here is Paris, yes, but here as in my bed, in my view, non non non; he is anywhere but here. It is too late for that now.

"Is he all right?"

"Oui, yes, as far as I know, as of this morning A is all right."

Well, he is alive. But who is she, Emily? Now he has another mess with another woman. God I hate women and I don't understand how I can never see it coming, not see "it" coming. I often see "it" coming, I like watching that, but this is the other it, the one that slams me in the face just when I believe in it, just when I think I am having it all -- why can't I see it? Maybe I do; I don't know, I don't know maybe I do and don't want to either, I am a complete naivete in love or I am sexually senile you would think I have enough experience to recognize all the signs, oh yes, every last sign by now, be wise by now but oh my god the older I get the younger I like them and the younger they are the crueler and more superficial they become, or is my skin just thinner? I'm just an odd old fart, just an odd old thin-skinned fart no wonder they hate me I hate myself. And these women of his always coming out of the woodwork.

"Who is calling?"

"Emily. Emily. His daughter."

"His what?"

I, I must sit down. Now I am not so thin-skinned that I can't be peeled away like an onion my head is spinning I can't be hearing what I'm hearing this is, this has absolutely to be the final surprise. Even my mind stops its usual babbling. I hastily pull myself together.

"His daughter. Who is your mother?"

"Jante. They lived together in Nice."

"Jante? Nice? Oh yes, yes, I seem to remember, a nice girl, that must be your mother, he had in Nice, Marseille, too, I think, yes, she left abruptly. Yes. No, he never told me about a child."

"She never told him."

"Oh, I see. He didn't, he doesn't, know yet either. Oh my, well, he is quite ill. Oh, you know--that's why Eduardo contacted your mother. Yes, well well, there is only one thing to do. You must come to Paris! A must meet you, before... well, you simply must come and stay here. Stay here in my apartment. It's huge -- you'll get lost. Don't pay for a hotel. Besides, it will be a little like having A here with me. You must come, will you come? Please, come, stay here with me."

EPISODE TEN

Emily and Eric

It's settled quickly, and my mother agrees with the plan.

I don't sleep much on the plane to Paris. I hope the anticipation of meeting Alec, my father, isn't palpable to the other passengers. They are oblivious to me. I re-read Mom's diary entry about her history with Alec; the one she gave me for my 17th birthday. It reads like one of her saucy purple prose short stories and I wonder if Life is really like that.

Eric is holding a sign with EMILY written in large, neat block letters and a generous bouquet of yellow roses.

"Eric?"

"Oui, M'sle." He kisses my hand and I stuff my face into the flowers for a brisk whiff of their perfume. I am expecting a younger man, a middle-aged man, and instead find a small elderly man, thin-legged with a jaunty paunch and a thinning head of white hair, a curious half smile.

"Let me…" I am reluctant to let an old man carry my bag, but he is energetic and carries himself with a youthful, dancing gait. Excitedly he speaks to me in stream of consciousness, as if I am inside his mind and reading his thoughts.

"I've told A about you -- well, as much as I know; it isn't much, you'll have to tell him all about yourself, only that well you're here. Wait! Let me look at you, s'il vous plâit! Mademoiselle! Arretez-vous for just a moment!"

Eric's China-blue eyes sweep over my face, my hair, my body, and I am suddenly shy like a gawky twelve-year-old girl, but also comfortable with his gaze, as if I am his patient and he is my doctor. I hope he is not disappointed. I also have the chance to look closely at him. A web of broken capillaries spreads from his nose to his cheeks; his thin lips form a crease across his jaw line.

"You have his mouth," he finally announces. I smile wide and chuckle. Eric adds, "But your face is open."

"His isn't?"

"A? Ah. No. A is a closed book of graces or dis-graces, an animal in a custom-made suit; a trickster, a liar, and a prince all in one, and don't believe anything he tells you. Have you been in Paris before?"

"Yes, well, I was here, once, for a semester, French class, high school. I didn't get much studying done."

"Hmm, a 'chip off the old block'."

We walk briskly, and I have to pick up my usual casual saunter to keep up with Eric.

"Too bad we didn't know you then; you could have met A, your father, under better circumstances oh, it doesn't matter; you're here now. You look about the right age, and you say Jante is your mother? I never met her I don't think she even knew I existed and maybe I met A about the time Jante left for New York. You were born in New York? And how is your mother?"

I don't feel he is really interested in hearing about my mother, so I switch the subject back to Alec, my father. "A."

"He is very ill. I wish you'd met him sooner he was so pretty, like a stealthy cat he made you want to put down a dish of warm cream so you could watch him lap it up."

It is almost impossible to talk when you first arrive in Paris. The graceful elegance of the city whispers of a secret, sensuous past and your mind wants only to drink it in, undistracted by small talk. We stay quiet in the cab, as I absorb the beauty of the city and we both absorb the enormity of what we are doing.

After settling in, Eric prepares tea, and as we sit in his large, baroque kitchen I ask Eric, "How did you meet Alec, my father?"

Eric walks me through the first steps of discovery. "A at first struck me with his totality in the moment how alive he made me feel. I became for the first time in years, maybe ever, and then how I fell under the illusion that I, foolhardy aristocratic dilettante that I am, or at least hope myself to be, could cultivate that, that? What is that? Spontaneity? now that's a word I hadn't heard in my circle in years, actually probably never; spontaneity, what a coarse thought. We are much too sophisticated to even understand the meaning of the word except as something that small children, very wee children in our circle, and of course animals, are capable of, but no one over the age of two and a half can even remember."

The enchantment of Paris and Eric's free association to everything "A" is both exhilarating and exhausting. We both agree I should take a long, deep nap before going to hospital to meet Alec for the first time. It is also a chance for Eric to prepare Alec for my arrival. I welcome the dark bedroom cloistered behind closed shutters and the silk eye mask he proffers as an essential accessory. From now on I will adopt the mask much the way Eric explains the cigarette holder he fondles and puffs on though he never lights the cigarette in it.

"I quit and adopted A as my drug of choice."

EPISODE ELEVEN

Eric

Emily -- Emily, A's child, how appalling! How unique! I love her instantly and she embodies A; too bad she is a girl, but she carries his genes, has his mouth, his wide delectable mouth, the way it stretches open wider when he comes; he never cries out, sometimes just a low grunt like a sailor tugging a line up through his throat. She is the first person who ever asked me how I met A. Her father, Alec, she calls him. I can't tell her all the details, of course not.

Yes, that's how it started, at a newsstand, one of those afternoon strolls just the beginning of spring, early March and there he is buying cigarettes, American cigarettes, Marlboro or Winston maybe Camels, furtively he looks at me for a split second while he hands over his francs which make a small tinkling sound into the Pakistani's hand while I offer him "a light" from my pocket lighter; always there, no better icebreaker I know of than that, no, none better than a cigarette. He offers me one all the while in the moment we both know the offer of the cigarette is an offer of much more, a secret password against which one can say yes or one can say no and while I prefer not to smoke I have learned its usefulness on these occasions. There was a time before A before I lost myself when I would just get so horny I'd walk through the streets and look at every man and put them into categories fuckable, fuckable in a crunch, not at all fuckable and oh yes many more fit into category one when I was horny than when I was not, but in those days I mostly was.

Simple you simple, simple, sensuous joy for me anyway at my age and A, half that, and yet what does it matter; funny for the older person in an affair, or so I thought of it that way, or "elder," which is really the age when you are fucking someone at least young enough to be your child and not those May December romances between a very rich old man and a girl his granddaughter's age who is in her own way probably crazy about him but let's agree if he was homeless she wouldn't be; such is life, but with A I also realize and accept and don't care, because after all I am getting such joy, such joy myself from his beautiful smooth hard young body that as long as long! as his cock becomes hard really hard that is all the proof I need or care about to believe that he too beside me he too receives his own joy from our encounters I don't have to analyze it.

Oh penis oh beautiful penis! – so alluring -- when it's small and soft like a delicate flower discreetly tucked away inside the tan shaft protected flower coquettishly virgin and the miracle! -- oh miracle! -- it is suddenly a manly thing its head as big as a cobra, its shaft stretched like a canvas over a frame and my tongue, my mouth, the artist's painterly brush stroking an invisible array of rainbow colors up over and about, it's either purpose-ly designed to entice me, fool me or otherwise totally innocently designed to receive pleasure wherever and from whoever it may arrive, its early escaping jewels wrapped into a sweet mucous stream plays into my mouth, a pungent sweet sticky string connecting the tip of my tongue with the tip of A's beautiful flower rod, the rest of his body too drawn as tight as skin can be on flesh, muscle, and bone, wrapped tightly inside a sinuous package.

There were days, oh I remember days before A be-fore my private addiction to A, oh I know I am hooked,

I know I am obsessed, I obsess oh god yes, but it isn't all my fault; it isn't just me and yet it is just me just the way I am, and A poor A just fell onto my tracks. On the other hand, A likes me this way; he does, he said so, he likes the way I am always there for him anytime, all the time, he just has to pick up the phone, ring the phone, come here now mister man and I'm there, oh I know he doesn't feel the same about me, I'm not that foolish I'm not fool enough to believe for a second that A has ever spent more than one minute thinking about me no less obsess about me, that would be out of the package, it is after all my job to obsess and his to be obsessed over but he likes the way I worry over him, mother him, I'm like a mother to him he says, and he can always depend on the money.

Sometimes luck travels with me and when I look a man right in the eye he looks back with the same hungry why not look sometimes he will pretend to ask directions and then I can pretend I am going that way myself here I'll show you. And when luck is with me I'll show him the way back to my apartment sometimes the luck is bad luck like the guy I sucked off and then he robbed me I was really pissed off about the blow job. And sometimes it is odd and comical, like the fellow who wanted to take a snippet of my hair, oh I still had my beautiful thick curls! as a souvenir of our tryst.

What did he do with it did he have snippets of every tryst's hair pinned in a collection, like old dead butterflies or pressed between the pages of a fat book like a dictionary or encyclopedia? And sometimes hilarious like the American who mimicked Maurice Chevalier thank heaven for little boys! That is how I met A walking down the street just like that.

And I notice immediately what is in front of me is definitely, eminently fuckable and if only I'd turned and walked away I'd have saved myself such pain, he was as wicked and delicious and not furtive but instead forward in his own covert way and I would never be the same, and would never take my strolls without secretly forever looking for A over and over and over again. He will always be my precious young idol my Eros and my doe.

I thought something wonderful has happened to me but infatuation always seems full of magic. Imagine this one person out of all the people on earth found me and now I am special, found not lost, I am found and touched as if by a wand and suddenly new again, born anew alive and wonderful. I've lost all my warts and my wounds are healed and I am seamless. It is full of wonder until the illusion dissipates and you are you again, and he is also small and lost, and even worse you have lost the little you finally gained because you decided to throw it all away. All the smartness, the savvy, the wisdom on this one small last chance that this irresistible young someone is going to throw it all away for you too! What fools we become. And when I threw it all away for A I lost what I used to have, what I managed over the precious years to put together for me: my self sufficiency, my self control, my self. My pride.

Oh and oh oh oh oh my, oh my god! I forgot what it was like I thought I was too old to ever feel that way again! And here it is! My skin having that hot sand feeling again, like a hot beach bitch in heat fire feeling again. Oh I know I am foolish, being really foolish to believe I'd never feel it again and way, way more foolish to feel it, that juicy saucy feeling that as long as there are young beautiful men on the planet I can still catch the young thing boy man, "I want you only you, can't live without you only like a hook to hang my hard on fever hat on.

And yet and yet and yet, there it is again, there it is again I am getting so used to it I hardly care anymore, a few crocodile tears and then, that's it. It's over. Maybe he got spooked oh what an old jerk I've become I was probably always a jerk, just a younger one or I must have imagined he was flirting with me just because, oh dear I was always flirting, always yearning for those moments of perfect passion perfect swashbuckling you've kidnapped my soul now I must surrender to you moments. Or maybe it was just that something "better" came along. I'm in love totally stupid moments, always imagined rarely in your lifetime realized.

And now here is A full of danger, and infectious.

A is the perfect instructor to teach me how to take rejection, how to "take it on the chin" of my heart that I wore on my coat for him. It is so obvious I adore him, he makes me feel, oh I don't even know anymore, all I know is what it feels like to be alone when sex is something more desired than achieved.

Men oh I know I am one but maybe at heart I am more like a woman. Men can be so unknowing so numb, blissfully ignorant of emotions and I have so many I trip over them. I am all grays. Most men have no subtlety no joy and yet I am one. We practice our clumsy unschooled dance steps when we are kind, at best, we try not to step on your toes. When unkind? Well never mind.

And yet and yet and yet. I am a man I carry this flesh around in my front pocket, little pathetic thing and oh yes, I have seen them strong and young and magnificent and oh yes, we can forgive them anything when they are like that but I am a little ashamed of being one of them. But then, how can women stand being themselves being women being so weird, so opposite unwieldy and convex, so other. Exotic but bizarre like the inside of a medina in Morocco, little hovels of busyness like a swarm of butterflies in the jungle, like the inside of a bathtub during a shower all splashy and wet like rainbows, colorful but without form. And also like a sandbox, gritty and full of tools for making gaudy and precious things that melt in the wind. Very strange creatures. I am glad I am not one of them.

And yet I am in some way like them, like a woman. Always wanting a man to do something, be something, prove something never just letting him be himself. Be something, be something to me for me baby, show me! I am the intermix, like a woman with all her quirky expectations and destinations planned and hoped for and also the man, the guy with the guy thing -- oh I have learned the hard way, no pun! -- that I am both terrified like a man and terrifying like a woman.

I admire heterosexual men dealing with women and their woman emotions, their woman dreams ,their vaginas. These men are fearless! But I don't recognize them, they are as alien to me as house plants, another species. And yet here is A, a man, oh god I can't forget his youthful splendor, his delicate aloofness and the coarse edge, the one he is working on smoothing out. And yet and yet! I also compare myself to the women I compete with and find they are better women and better men than I am. I don't know what I blame myself for when I am rejected, I blame myself as if I am the only one to blame, the old jerk. Maybe it's not me? Maybe there is just something wrong with my choices, not me. I wonder if I were a woman would the choices be better wiser smarter and I gather not, I think the only people with choices are young men with big cocks and young girls with wet cunts but only if they know the value of these things. I remain stolidly a flaccid old unmarketable and unremarkable jerk. Young men in their own concave ignorant way are jerks in the making, we all are when it comes to sex and forget love we are fooling ourselves, we are either successful missionaries or merely milkmen toting the product and hoping for customers and with a little luck, building a route. But you can stick that hard boy cock in there anytime you want to anytime. There's nothing like sex to solve the same problems with one hand while spewing forth with the other.

EPISODE TWELVE

Eric and A

Okay. Let me stop. Catch my breath. I am enthralled with A's in my face spontaneity and yet I have tried -- tried! -- without any apparent success to cultivate him -- let me not kid myself, train him -- to be my pet, my grateful ever allegiant always there for me never petulant pet. Instead I discover an impetuous young and arrogant -- though not angry! -- human not about to be anyone's pet. Rough around the edges yet smooth, hard. To my chagrin he stands up to me, stands up for himself while I, old fool at my age am left staring incredulously at a blank wall, waiting for the writing to appear on it. The blank wall that remains after one of our arguments or after one of my unanswered phone calls and most certainly after one more of our unkept-by-A dates.

I have to appreciate the following: A is not essentially homosexual and I am. A lives in the moment and I don't know where I live, in the past? in the future? Or, some parallel universe that is more like an architectural rendering than real life, I live in an illustration of life like a blind person or an autistic constantly looking for patterns that I can discern and trust, A is the paint in the illustration, the colors the background, the figures walking through what for me are artificial streets. Me looking for the rabbit hole, the looking glass that will toss me into an experience that I can actually touch, where A is the three- dimensioned artist's hand that reaches through the canvas and touches me and brings me to life, where he is the cartoonist and I am the cartoon figure.

It should have been the other way around he was to be the Eliza to my Professor Higgins but instead he is the one who shows me how to be charming, how to be engaging, how to master elocution and through elocution speak beautiful lies.

So here I am disassembling the truth, for him! The truth is A lives in the moment and manipulates it while in the moment with me convinces me that I am wholly a part of his life and he will be there again for me just as we planned the next day, three days from now, in fact once he leaves my sight his life overtakes him and pitiful me I am "waiting in the wings" for my part to begin. And instead of me there is an understudy filling in for me and I am merely left waiting and my hold on reality then is to analyze how I came to be there waiting. Waiting and hoping at my age what an old fool I have become! so here I am an old fool waiting for the brash young smooth hard thing to sweep back into my life and inject me with reality, save me from my stupid architectural rendering and return the third dimension to me -- no, return me to it. And the very quality of his life that makes that possible -- his ever in the moment taking life for what it is quality that forces me, allows me to once again participate as a player, not just sitting in the bleachers -- is the very same quality that distracts him completely from me, makes him forget I exist. Certainly, while he may be young and foolhardy, I am much older and simply foolish.

I find equilibrium in my small safe rituals, like pouring an elegant flute of sherry and holding it up to the light and then my ties, tidying my ties straightening them smoothing them as if they are the most important things in the world, placing an order for delivery of dry cleaning anything, anything at all to distract me from the fact of my empty rendered existence and keeping at bay the imagined real life A is living, probably with someone else right now -- probably even worse with a woman.

The thing is he fits me 'like a glove' -we agree on that- like the pair of fine kid gloves I bought for him. When I bring them for him I place one of them on his right hand and then I take his hand and place it on my member and make him stroke it with the glove on as if it is a second skin on his fingers and as if I am what I don't know, just a lonely old fool though I don't know it at the time, I still think I can be the puppeteer.

I buy him new clothes, why, because I want to see him in them and also because I want to brush him with 'haute monde' in case I run into friends while I am with him though certainly Gregory and François would not care what he is wearing, they will mentally undress him anyway and understand what I have there.

He tries them all on for me, I like the new sweaters especially the soft chestnut one that matches his eyes, they all looked stunning especially since he had nothing else on, I appreciate his uncircumcised penis when I lie on my back and he kneels over me and I pull the tawny skin up and over the head so that it forms a little bud and then I pull it back to reveal the rosy ripe fruit which I place my mouth fully around and suck the sweet juice from and swallow.

And of course Gregory and François do mentally undress him when they run into us at the bar.

"How cute," one of them says, "What a darling young... "

Thing, body, boy? A is more than those adjectives, no one can easily put him into one word, one crude sound, he is something more than a word or a sound can describe and yet he is also just a sound, a grunting breathy frustrated sound, as if you want to describe him in a syllable and yet you can't find the right combination of sounds in a single syllable to define him, or to find the sound that describes your own instinctual sexual response hunger feeling about him. As if he is a sight, a smell, a kind of food that one remembers from childhood or sooner, something even more primal, like the odor of birth or even the womb.

When I leave my business meetings today I feel okay, he hasn't called yet though he had promised to for dinner and I think he will call so that we could set our appointment for tonight but I am feeling okay that he hasn't called, a date is sort of a bother after all isn't it? I stop in a café to order dinner to take home with me and the young man behind the counter has his sleeve turned up toward the elbow like A does and I can see he has the same upper body build and skin as A and the unquenchable hunger stings me.

These are the worst moments, when I am expecting him, when he doesn't call, when I can't reach him when I think he is with someone else, probably a woman! when I realize how old and foolish I have become and how hopeless, I look at myself in the mirror checking wrinkles slathering on the expensive age-defying creams hoping for the best. Praying actually that there will be just one last moment in which to throw myself headlong into the headlights of an oncoming car, the driver a handsome young hunter and me an old deer -- old dear! -- out for that last dangerous leap across the highway, one last chance for salvation or destruction the real risk being left with just a damaged crippled and not dead carcass. And then the years of suffering while obsessed with a young virile beautiful male who has no consciousness or loyalty to anyone. I am stupid blind old and now lost, waiting I feel like I am a lady in waiting as if I am fanning myself looking teasingly out from behind my fan waiting and how ridiculous! I am not a pretty feminine waiting thing in a corset and silk dress. I am an old hairy male and even worse, cynical really cynical except for this young vital man that I am hanging by a thread for hoping for, I don't even know what maybe if I'm really lucky a pass at that beautiful flower bud, a little bite of that sweet succulent fruit. Even just a word of encouragement.

When A does come in I put my take-home dinner aside, I'm not really hungry after all, not for food, for A yes famished but not for food and when he comes in he looks so delicious I want to eat him like pastry. "Comme ça va?" I try on my best nonchalance for him. "Where have you been?"

"I ran into some friends. From Marseille." Friends? Gay men? Straight men? Women? I don't know which I fear the most. Still wearing my nonchalance, pulling it up around my throat , buttoning it up tugging at its sleeves to button them up too, "Oh, friends? That's nice." How nonchalant, "Huh, from Marseille, too, such a small world."

A has taken off his jacket and shirt and I want to lick his chest his small hard nipples, I want to feel his flesh next to mine but he just dresses again, this time in the soft chestnut sweater that is my favorite.

"Not really. I ran into them on the train from Marseille, on my way here. We'd made plans to meet. I'm meeting them again, we're going to dinner, I just came back to change.

Plans, I don't understand, I thought we had a date.

"I don't understand, I thought we had a date." My beautiful nonchalance begins to unravel.

"I'm sorry. I forgot. I mean, I didn't know you were counting on it."

Counting on it? Oh no, why would I, old village

idiot with receding hairline and expanding paunch, be counting on it? On you?

"Oh, uh, no. No, it was just a thought, just a casual thing..." I lie so badly that for a hair of a moment I even believe he will take pity on me, say, god what was I thinking, I didn't realize how much you want me, my friends can wait.

"Can you do me a favor?"

"Yes?" Kiss me before I go?

"Can you give me some cash?"

The least I can do. I tuck 2000 francs into his jacket's upper pocket and he gives me a little smile and a peck on the cheek.

"Thanks, I'll see you later."

And when he walks out the door my beautiful nonchalant robe falls into a pile of loose threads at my feet and I gather them into my hands and press them into my face and I cry, there in the foyer of my apartment and sob and hope the neighbors can't hear me. I only console myself realizing there are so many other fools, men and women just like me now and ever, who have succumbed to the smooth hardness and languished in the stupidity of last chances at love, some of them lucky enough not to have survived the crash.

That night, when A comes in I can tell he has been drinking, but that is good for me because he comes into my room wearing just the chestnut-colored sweater and puts his penis in front of my face and says. "Lick it. Do it. Put it in your mouth." And I do. The sweet tawny bloom; the rosy fruit. All mine. All of you.

I walk to my office the next morning without brushing my teeth. I want to hold onto the sticky tangy taste of A's come, even meeting with a client -- oh, my clients! gratefully rich patrons who depend on me year after year, "Eric, I really can't stand that old chaise in the parlor another day, Eric, dear, you really must do something about the lighting in the library, it's dismal" -- they trust me as if I am their doctor and I love them as one would eccentric aunts and uncles or naughty pets but I am eager to finish up early so I can shop for A, what will it be today? Soft Italian leather shoes? I smell the leather and am aroused to link the smell of the leather with A's erotic sweaty aroma when he has had an orgasm. Egyptian cotton sheets? Lush bath towels, silk shirts? I decide on the silk bathrobe, a filmy cranberry-colored fantasy, my fantasy and I imagine the tawny rosebud peering out from between its bloody colored opening. I pick up a bottle of Veuve Clicquot its orange label and Madame Clicquot's visage, a symbol of what I desire of A, what I expect to happen he is always friendlier with two or three glasses of champagne, I pretend to sip along with him but really I am watching the sweet biting bubbles take their effect on his mood, there, now a little softer around the corners, the hard edge brightening to a warm pinkish glow, before I bring out today's present I am so sure he will be pleased.

"Eric, I wish you would stop buying me things."

"What?" I am confounded. "I, I, I don't under-stand, I, I, I was, I am just trying to please you, I'm just trying to be nice to you. I, I thought you liked presents."

"I do, Eric. But your gifts are like a loaded weapon."

I am stung again -- oh when will I learn, when will I be realistic, when will I get it straight with this boy, this boy man who I adore, whose sex is my drug my drug yes that's what he is I can't free my thoughts of him my entire day wraps around the evening when I will see him, I am also getting panicky he is leaving Paris again soon, going back to that plain jane of a woman that shadow that mere mirror of a man's idea of a total person, she waits on him, picks up after him, oh I do too, A haven't you noticed how I lavish my world on you, what do you see in her she is just a boring figment of a human, and a woman, no less just a woman, and not even a very pretty one at that. Or maybe it is that fat old whore living off her rich husband at the Negresco. Or, who knows?

"What do you see in her, anyway?"

"She's kind. She leaves me alone. She takes care of

me and doesn't crowd me."

"I, I don't crowd you, do I?"

"You are very crowded, Eric."

"But I don't feign weakness, like the women in your life, just waiting in the shadow for the right moment to pounce, to get control of you."

"I don't know. Maybe you're right. I don't understand women."

"What's there to understand. They're evil. They can't be trusted."

I pause here, to gather my arguments, my time with A is piddling away, if only I could keep him here!

"But you're not happy with her."

"Happy?" Alec peers into the bubbles. "I don't know. What is happy?" he queries and looks at me. "What about you, Eric, are you happy?"

"Me. Well, yes, yes, when you're here with me, I think I am." I second guess myself but continue, "Yes. Then, yes, I am happy, when you're here with me." I am, I am, I am so happy when it is just A and me, just talking, sensibly, openly. "Why don't you try it on?"

A sighs and puts down his glass as he gets up. "All right. But later. I'm going out now. When I come back tonight, I'll put it on for you."

Wearing the new robe that night A explains, "I was attracted to you, at first, because your mind was, well,

it was a place of such rigor. Such vice. I loved its tough-
ness and intelligence. But frankly, Eric, you went soft.
I don't mean physically..."

That too, I silently add to fill in A's reportage.

"I mean your mind. The one thing that really attracted me to you." Pause. "It went soft." Large pause.
"And frankly, I hate to say it. Sour."

But A, oh I forged the iron of my disappointment on
A's long series of small rejections. Eric you want me too
much oh didn't I know it of course I do you are my angel
and my last chance at love, Eric the more you try to hold
me the more I want to get away -- oh yes! of course I know
this but I feel my own luck my own youth escaping with
you I wonder if there was ever anyone in your life you
needed too much, who hammered your hope into nails.

Sour, sour oh god I hate myself now I know I really
do more than I ever did and god knows I've had my
bouts but sour, sour like old cabbage I might as well be
dead I wish I was dead I might as well be an old rotted
out piece of fruit garbage just smelly so no one wants
to even walk on it, it might make the bottom of their
shoes smelly, disgusting, sour now I know the worst
name I've ever been called I'd rather be called dead at
least that comes with respect.

"Sour? Is that the best you can say to me? You're so
cruel to me." I love you.

EPISODE THIRTEEN

Eric

After the diagnosis, everything suddenly becomes "before" or "after" I don't, nobody does, none of us know can ever imagine, or would have believed a scourge a royal fucking scourge like this ever, ever how can it, we just became free began freeing ourselves coming out all the way out and now this. Why A? Indeed Why A and why not me? Of course I go for the tests we all do as soon as you heard but you know in the early days we don't even know what to ask for what test, test what, "My friend, you know, my friend has, you know he's 'sick...'"

I, we, the doctors don't have a name and god forbid you go to the wrong doctor a straight one they are all around us then doctors nurses who think you are contagious especially as the rumors spread and they do before the facts thank god! Among my friends among us there were doctors known to be sympathetic or gay themselves, probably some infected who weren't afraid to draw our blood be frank who came armed with facts instead of fear and who would tell the truth. In the beginning we had mysterious words, definitions hinted not spoken the name not said, like cancer in the 1950s undefined before it became called by its name and doesn't aid mean help? Something in the naming though, something about giving it a name defined it, pinned it to the wall like a hunted specimen but too late too late too much damage, too many friends lovers strangers, too many lost.

For a while the news stories focus on singling out a cause, Haiti oh yes Haiti yes now there's a good cause a good source of this evil especially Haitian men, black men among the poorest in the world and then it was the sailor the great white hope! a white man's disease after all it can't be all that bad! a single white sailor where did he bring it from, Africa probably the news media would want it that way better that way than monkeys, African monkeys of course were the source and maybe the sailor caught it by having intercourse with an ape. The tests became easier to find and more routine, I know what to ask for places where it is easy (easy!) to walk in and get tested only the waiting for results is hard, when the anxiety gnaws at you and you make deals: I promise this time I really promise no more chances no more unsafe sex I promise, and the walks down the street become more and more clandestine, less frequent and far more menacing.

After the diagnosis something changes in A, something beautiful something luminous as if his smooth hard surface turned to clear alabaster and a light shines through it to the surface from below and suddenly A -- the amusing manipulative A-- has a soul and it illumines his skin and his eyes, it inhabits his limbs his torso his mouth, his wicked smiling mouth, as if the old A had already died and this new one, a point of heat, a gift, from the universe alights here in my life like an exotic bird from another world I am so gratified A finally needs me. It is my home, my refuge after his tests, before he denies what it all means, when my love for A is finally fully realized, I can stop yearning and simply give up to him. He is broken, a lost little boy afraid and unsure. Unlike the A who took my gifts my money and desires and snubbed them out like a cigarette, this A is real and while he stays with me he regains his physical strength and taps into a pool of spirit he hadn't known before and he leaves me again, but not without giving me back my own soul, the one that doesn't depend on A for my survival or happiness.

EPISODE FOURTEEN

Emily and Alec

The French cabbie refuses to "comprendre" my poor French and so I draw him a map of where the hospital is located. The hospice entrance is on a small, shaded side street, off the traffic. A squat lady under a barren shawl sells small posies of wilted flowers that she tries to press into my hand.

The hospital is vintage 19th-century and I half expect to see nurses in winged caps fly through the antiseptic corridors, singing. I am directed to my father's room. Each step that takes me to him awakens my awareness, as if I am hallucinating. My nervousness strangely dissipates as I enter his room and I hear Eric speaking.

"I was reflecting on my life last night…"

"Oh really?"

I see Alec for the first time, half sitting up in the bed, loyal Eric at his side. I expect to find a handsome young suitor but instead find a man depleted of his youth and vigor.

"We are so different, A. You lived your life as if it were a great high wire performance. To me it's just one big clown act."

"Since when have you been reflective, Eric?', Alec asks jocularly.

I stand inside the doorway, Alec and Eric eyeing me over without disrupting their insider ribbing.

"Sometimes I am!"

I will learn to love Eric. Patient, aging, devoted Eric. Alec is much too real for me yet; I don't know how I am going to feel about him. While they speak, Alec is looking deep, deep into me like a crystal ball that should give him answers.

"You must be Emilia." Alec's smooth accent rolls my name out lyrically through a mouth that looks like my own, but more disciplined, more like a zipper than the piano mine has been compared to, as if no word could ever escape between his lips that weren't scripted in his mind before sliding out between them.

"Emily." I correct him. Emilia, I repeat to myself.

"She has your mouth."

"Emilia. Please. Sit here." Alec pats the side of the bed. I am afraid but sit there as told. My head swarms and I want to run away from this beehive of feelings, but I am determined instead to just fit in. Alec reminds me of a stray alley cat, gazing at me, calmly, and I don't want to introduce any sharp gestures that might frighten him away. He says "join us" in a way that welcomes me into the private club that is Alec and Eric's own secret world.

In a mockingly serious psychiatrist tone Alec tells me, as if I am their longest-lost friend, "Eric was just about to reflect on his life for us. Just so you know, Eric hurls himself rashly, heart first into everything, especially love. He never reflects. He obsesses."

"But I do reflect! I swear it -- last night, for instance..."

"What great insights did you ..."

I notice that Alec, my father, has the ability to interrupt Eric's train of thought speaking.

"Eric always thought I was the one who lived in the moment..."

"...you were calculating..."

"I was calculating. But go on. Reflect. Please. Amuse us. Emilia may as well get to know your reflective side, too."

Eric looks at me and asks, "May I speak freely?"

And I nod, though he doesn't pause for my answer

and continues headlong, "Well, all the men in my life, I do reflect on them a lot. .."

"So now you're reflecting on all of them instead of obsessing on one of them." Alec is speaking to Eric but looking at me. "Especially me."

"Well yes, that's true, you are the most fabulous object of my obsessive mind, a driving passion." "Driven," Alec corrects. Eric explains to me, "…but last night -- well, last night I was thinking of them all, how layered like a gold mine like a rich archeological dig, like history itself."

"Don't get carried away…", Alec ribs. "It's just your own personal history, Eric."

"No, really, the lovers in my life are like layers of skin like an onion. Lance belongs to the layer I call friend but also had sex with only occasionally, never any strings attached and no obsessing allowed; Nitya was my private Kama Sutra -- oh, he was very sensuous very attentive to detail, Paul was a business associate -- amiable, very amiable, we could always get a little in the men's room and Guillaume destined to love me always though that *was* a very long time ago, but we never forget the one who loved us the most, right, A? and then there was Jean you remember Jean, so jovial, uncertain, afraid, concerned about cleanliness, actually very neurotic, even more neurotic than me, and Martin, so terrified of being queer! I wonder if his wife ever found out and then," he adds with a deep wistful sigh, "all those whose names I've forgotten or never bothered to learn, but I can still see their faces!"

"And their cocks. And they're probably all dead now," reflects Alec. "And what about me?"

"A. A. A. You are my mirror image another one with too many choices--oh yes, here you are, here I am, the other one who can't discriminate."

"Emilia." Eric adopts my new identity. "Am I being too gauche?" I am giggling by now, and Eric takes this as incentive to continue. "I had a system of flirtation, when I was much younger, of course..."

"Eric, admit you wish you could still use it!"

"... not aggressively, not as I used to; it's all in my mind now, and I seem to remember you liked learning this system yourself, A, and employed it with much success. In any case, Emilia I took seven steps," and here Eric clears his throat and uses his fingers to very deliberately count out the steps of his dance of seduction.

"One. I note everyone in the room. Two. I note everyone in the room who notices me. Three. I screen those and place them each in a category: look back, ignore, pursue, be oblivious, second choice. Four. Choose to pursue. Five. Check the response. Six. Pursue. Seven. Heaven."

"What about eight?" I ask him.

"Eight?" They both laugh, and Eric says, "We never thought about eight!"

Alec explains, "It would be like a hunter picking up the still-warm helpless thing he just shot and looking it in the eye."

Intrigued with the system and desperate to belong, I say, "You don't have to explain this system. I use one like it, too. I never thought about it so logically."

"You *are* my mirror image," Alec says to me and looks me over more carefully now. "Fairest of them all."

I am flattered to think he may think I am fair, attractive.

Eric adds, "An Alice in Wonderland image, I might add -- down the rabbit hole for you! It's true that age, class, and money are like costumes, but backstage, alone, we look at each other and laugh; we are our own private carnival. We never thought about eight"

"That is," muses Alec, "until I became ill."

EPISODE FIFTEEN

Alexandro.
Alec. A.

The next day, Eric busies himself with "work" and "chores" to give me the opportunity to spend time alone with Alec.

Alec is turned on his side and his face rests on a thin, starchy institutional pillow. Still, it is a pillow, and his head on it seems so natural as if he were born to be in bed, not in an office or working behind a counter. In bed. So he would die here. In a bed, his head on a pillow, seeking some point on the horizon, some place not connected with my life, or anyone's, even his own. For the first hour I mainly sit aside him while he rests.

I am startled when he suddenly speaks to me.

"I've never told anyone this before. I don't think. Well, maybe one other person. One lover. Probably Rae. I told Rae everything--well, almost everything. But never anyone, not anyone, not anyone like you, like a real person in my life. Not a friend. Not family."

Alec looks toward the window, instead of straight ahead, instead of at me, at the ceiling, at some undefined point in space and time. He pauses and ponders the word, as if it is a prism catching the sun light. "Family." I, too, look at the word and am struck by its myriad rainbows.

"Not even Eduardo." He takes a deep breath and pulls himself up on his knobby elbow, and then leans back as if he is my patient and I've just asked him about his childhood.

"I never really thought about dying. I mean, not real dying. I always thought of dying when I had sex. No, no, not quite true. I thought of dying when I was about to have an orgasm when I was thinking about coming."

Thinking about coming. I didn't realize before this moment that thinking was something that a person might be doing before having an orgasm; I thought it was the opposite--one stops thinking.

Another pause. I wonder why Alec, my father, feels this is something he has to confess, clear the air

116

about, before he dies, I mean, really dies. It is clear he doesn't view me as his daughter. Yet, he claims me in some fashion as his confessor, as if I am another part of himself, cut off from him, like a shank or a bone he had amputated from his body that would somehow wondrously transform itself into another, second life for himself. Like a rib.

"…You know, I had my first sexual experience with a woman, older, no, not just any a woman. She was my mother's best friend, Fanny. To me though -- I was twelve -- she was a goddess! What did she see in me? I was just a scrawny boy. But it happened just after my mother died. I guess she thought I was lonely. Well, I was." He pauses, and adds, " Shattered."

I am quieter than I have ever been in my life. Whenever my mother would go into one her reveries, it was usually after a few glasses of wine, and I'd learned to dread the stories of her past hopes, and especially her references to Alec, my father. When I was very young, I couldn't hear enough of her stories of Alec -- I felt I'd had to dig into her and drag them to her surface -- but over time, the stories became mechanical and I stopped listening. Now I am listening to Alec himself, but instead of my mother he is talking of his own, my grandmother, and I am hearing of her for the first time.

"My mother. Pretty Giselle. Pretty, crazy Giselle.

Her death. Was it an accident? Suicide? Fate? I've never been able to decide..." He sighs, a deep, endearing sigh. He is my father, after all. I can't ignore his plaintive solitude. "But her death... it's all connected.. .the two...it's funny, I never really connected the two...sex...death.... Giselle would have been so angry with Fanny."

"La petite morte?" I ask. That much I remember from high school French.

"Oui. Non, non. Le grande. Grande Morte. Not the little death, not just a little orgasm. The real thing. That's what was in my mind...just before...you know, those few seconds just before... when your mind decides, no it doesn't decide, it finally stops deciding, what path, the safe one? No, orgasm. The slippery one, yes, come, let go, the moment of vulnerability. Well then... in those tense few seconds, half seconds before, my decision was whether or not I would walk to the catapult, the edge of the cliff... would I leap? Yes. No. Yes. Yes because for me that was the crucial fantasy. Death. Yes. Leap. Yes. Off the cliff. Off the edge. Into death. The free fall. Flying."

"La grande morte..."

At this, Alec, my father, looks me in the eye, for the first time, in this reverie, maybe ever, as if he really did see his mirror image and his confessor, his biographer, all in one.

"Yes."

Well, it isn't surprising that Alec, my father, now lay in a bed, his head sunken like a rock in sand, dying of a disease, a dreadful pestilence, spread through sexual freedom and perhaps his own sexual prowess. And excess.

"Too bad," Mom once wrote for the university's press "that as we evolved our cultural indulgence of open sex, we pushed the edge of the unseen, virulent world, there, right on our heels, waiting for us to screw our brains out, waiting in its own microscopic staging ground to exploit our weaknesses for its own survival."

Alec paused, winced; it wasn't possible to track all his current sources of pain, and continued, "It's funny comparing men and women. The way they decide to have sex, or not. I love women. I am enamored of them. Enthralled. But men are so much easier to read than women. Yes. Yes to sex. Yes, now. Yes is just painted in their eyes, body language, je ne sais quoi, women, women, are so coy, so stratified. When? Maybe. It's so hard to know what they mean. Are they saying yes? No? Who knows, I don't think they know themselves. So it was much easier to have that fast getting it on sex, with men, with a man. I could walk down the street, pass a man, and know, in an instant, yes, we can go off in a doorway right now, and well, do it, whatever it was at the moment, *maintenant.*

"Isn't that how you met Eric?"

"Oh, he told you? How much did he tell you? Never mind…I will have no secrets from you, my little offspring," he confides, and continues his comparison between men and women.

"With women, it never happens like that, unless they are whores 'going out?' The faster the better -- just say yes and pay first. With most women, though, there are complications. What's your name. Where do you live. Where are you from? What do you want in your life, you must want something. Do you want me, for more than, well, you know, more than just sex. Will you give me babies? Will you support us? Will I die alone or will you be there for me? When I am old, gray, wrinkled, ugly, fat. Can you live with my family, will they like you? Who is your family, what are they like, do you like them, do they like you? Will you betray me? All these questions, passing through a woman's mind, all in the first few moments of conversation."

Occasionally Alec, my father, glances at me, to see if I am listening or if I am bored. Sometimes his eyes are suddenly clear and they pierce through me. And then they are gray and glazed and looking far away to a point on a horizon I can't see. When the evening nurse enters, she tugs at the curtain separating his bed from the window. I peck my lips tentatively to his forehead. Though gaunt from his disease he is still handsome, or at least his youthful good looks are still detectable, an arresting mix of boy and man, of vigor and death.

I am both riveted and repulsed by his stories. I don't want to know the intimate, sordid details of my father's life. But here I am, wanting to learn what I can from him, about him, and these are the only details he is willing to share. Maybe these are the only details he has to share. Maybe because it is the cause of his decay, maybe the only thing that ever mattered to him. Maybe, as my mother suggests, Alec only experienced sensation; maybe the normal range of human emotion is outside his reach. Maybe because of my own ambiguity, my own sexual curiosity, I am keenly interested in finding clues to my own life in his.

Alec closes his eyes, and when I leave him and walk past the nurses' station, their tinkering sounds and low voices remind me of birds in a bird bath. On the street the heat and the traffic sound woolly and embrace me, and I am silent.

The next day, I bring him brilliant yellow tulips from the flower lady, tulips the color of egg yolks. He barely acknowledges them, but they cheer the room, and me.

He has a visitor, Rae. Rae is dressed in an elaborate

woman's outfit, striking sunglasses, and a flouncy red wig. She is beautiful, but her Adam's apple gives away her birth gender. Rae describes life with Alec in an exaggerated stage whisper that embarrasses me; I am certain Alec can hear Rae, and worse, knows I am listening. And worse yet, I can feel real or feigned sympathy for Rae, but it is awkward.

"I lived with him -- for a year-- I knew, I knew all the while I knew -- he was positive -- and I had unprotected sex with him! Thank God!! –course we didn't know the --- I'm not, still not-- and then!! you know and then -- he left me. For someone else! He left. Went to a beach house in --I don't remember where. Honey, he left me! We had so much, I was making money in those days, we had a Mercedes together. He left me, with nothing, no money, a year! For a real woman! But you know what, he came back-- they always come back, he came back! A year and a half later -- guess what -- knock knock knock -- on my door there he was - back and you know what I said? Fuck you."

Rae accentuates this remark with an arm gesture and an ugly facial expression. I listen intently, I want to hear, know everything I can about Alec's life that I can glean, and have to rely on the people he has surrounded himself with. Strange people. Strange Alec. He is a puzzling mix of signals. And he is being made delirious by the disease that is killing him. And do I hope that in knowing Alec, my father, I will learn to grasp myself? I suppose. I am learning more than I want to know.

How will I explain all this to Jante?

Rae hasn't been back since his disclosure to me about his year of unprotected sex and his extraordinary luck at not having contracted the virus. I wonder at the death wish Rae harbors, to take such a chance; it is like stepping in front of a moving vehicle and daring the driver to run you over. Not once, but every day.

I am sitting bedside when Alec wakes up. He reaches for a glass of water, and I reach at the same time and our hands self-consciously touch, when he continues his comparison of men and women.

"I know it sounds self destructive, it does to me now, but I always loved danger. Look at Uncle Eduardo. He always lived a risky life, adventurous, daring, on the edge. And danger mixed up with sex is the greatest adventure of all." I get a little queasy and wonder if this is some kind of strange incest, this story telling, my father's exhibitionism, my voyeurism. But I identify with the analogy of sex and danger. Love and death. It reminds me of my own closeted teenage jaunts with strangers on Rockaway beach when my mother thought I was just innocently taking a walk in the dark.

Alec continues, "…Men are more dangerous than women, men, well, they're brutish, they're aggressors…"

I add, "…And maybe, maybe this one is the ax murderer."

Alec chuckles at the irony.

"I thought my killer would be bigger than me; instead my killer is detectable only by someone in a lab coat. Can I have some more water?"

I hold the cup for him and this time his hand clasps mine, around the glass, weakly. I can't figure out if Alec understands or believes that I really am his offspring and wonder if there are others. Half-sisters, half-brothers, Alec's eyes, his mouth, my mouth. And while I know it to be a fact in my own case, paternity and the reality of Alec are very remote cousins. I venture deeper into Alec's psycho-sexual landscape by asking him if women were ever dangerous?

"Women? Oh my lord, no, no. Never. They were my refuge, they were where I went when I needed to go home, home to 'Mommy.'"

"What about Giselle, I mean, my grandmother, did she make you feel safe?

Alec visibly squirmed, as if adjusting a hat for church, or a tie for an important business meeting.

"I don't remember her much anymore. I know she was pretty. And sometimes, very nervous. Sometimes she made me nervous. I don't think I was afraid her, ever. Nervous? Yes, sometimes, nervous."

"But did you feel safe with her?" I asked, my Psych 101 getting into the fray.

Alec sighed. "I felt safe, most safe, with my father. My mother, Giselle, my uncle, Eduardo, they were too exciting; I was always a little excited, nervous, with them, as if things could get away from us, and as if we could get away, away from everything, even danger..."

"And that felt dangerous...?"

Alec paused, now, closed his eyes, exhausted. "Yes, yes. I don't know why I did the things I did. It just happened, I don't know..."

I peck his forehead again -- it is cool to my lips -- and pull the covers up to his throat.

I leave him and wander alone through the narrow, back streets of Paris. The old buildings stand guard over each intersection, stepping back off the corner as if to let the traffic pass, their soft antique façades and cornices like fancy pastries carved from stone. Each door presents its own unique face to visitors, huge ornate steel portals staunchly challenging all to think twice before entering. Paris may be the most romantic city in the world, but I am eager to get back to New York, back to my own reality and New York's determined indifference. Paris is like Alec's women, enveloping and forgiving, while New York is like his men, caustic, sarcastic and maybe deadly.

I don't know if Alec's death is imminent, or if he will rally. What if I leave and he dies the next day -- will I have abandoned him? Why do I care? He was a father who was not a father, who was barely, remotely, and only lately certain of my existence. Would he even notice I was gone?

EPISODE SIXTEEN

Emilia and Alec

In the morning I walk into my father's room and find him sitting erect. He is groomed, clean-shaven, his hair thinly brushed back and the vestige of his youthful, healthy good looks stares at me with a hard, clean edge I hadn't yet seen in him. In all our meetings so far, he has rested like a tired willow branch on his pillows, dreamy and distant, reflective, cagey and flirtatious. This morning he directs his attention to me, as if he has become the reporter.

"And what do you want in your life, Emilia?" I am startled. I expected to be the prompter again, coaxing his secret life from within those skinny ribs.

"I, uhh..." What do I want? For once I know I can,

know I have to, give an honest answer, but I hesitate, stammer. "Well, just, I don't know... well, I, well, I just, well...maybe, I just want to be in love."

There. Said.

"Is there someone in particular you want to be in love with? Is there someone you have in mind?"

"No, oh no! I just want to know that you can, or that I can, I know you can..."

"Can I...?"

"I mean, I just want to be in love for a more than minute, or an hour, or a week, I want to be in love for a long time, I see what it does to people..."

"You do...?"

"I mean, look at my mother...""

"Your mother, is she?"

"I mean she's been in love with you all these years."

"She has...?

I can't believe I've told him that. Jante will kill me.

He reflects on this thought with a fretful sigh, goes on to explain.

"Well, you know, mi Emilia, love is a negotiation. It changes. After falling 'out of love' that's when the real work begins. Love evolves with each moment, but especially, with each choice you have to make together. What do you want to have for dinner, where shall we go this weekend, whom shall we be friends with, which side of the bed, the fan or the air conditioner? Who will wash the dishes, who will pick up the clothes? The top or the bottom? It's a constant negotiation. It's exhausting work. And then you have to layer in the less obvious, 'Who am I as a person and if we decide to go ahead together, what kind of freak will that make us -- that weird disjointed yet conjoined thing called a couple." He may as well have added "Yuck." I guess Alec, my father, is not the best role model for marriage.

"And finally there is that 'Is it me, something I've done, said? Failed to do stage. Or is it you, have you failed? Better it's you'. At best, we agree it is a simple matter of communication. And we figure it out. Come out with a plan that fixes it for both of us. Ah yes, I needed too much. Ah yes, I got disenchanted. Let's fix it. Let's practice and get it better next time. Okay, then, worse. It's over, at least for one of us. We are done. One of us is too thin or too fat, too simple or complicated, too needy, too loose, too, too, too. But when that happens, 'I will tell you. Just tell you.' The cold like a sharp knife right through the flesh, to the bone truth. Bone to steel. But, of course, they never do. You always have to find it out the hard way. In daily bad-tasting doses. Until it is finally obvious the patient is dead."

He stops here, satisfied he has dissected and eviscerated Love and skewered it once and for all. He adds, "Truth is best."

He ponders this idea for a moment. "It's just simpler."

And then asks me, "Do you have a lover?"

Funny he says lover. American fathers would ask if I have a boyfriend.

"Well, there's Angel. Angel is the closest thing I have to a boyfriend, or a lover."

And then he oddly adopts a severe tone and I'm not sure if he is mocking or really trying to take on the role of the protective father. "Who is Angel?"

And then realizing his tone has taken me by surprise, modulates the question. "I mean, what is Angel like?"

"He's kind of short, but good looking, very good looking, very smart, very sexy, and he has a good heart…"

"But?" He adds, "Is he an angel?" I roll my eyes in response.

"Well, he's really immature. Not that I don't sometimes act like an eight-year-old, but he just acts out most of the time, like a spoiled boy. He's selfish and acts like he's entitled to everything and then he gets upset when things don't go his way -- right away! - - and then when he doesn't live up to his responsibilities he makes excuses! Always excuses! And, he…"

Alec graciously comments, " … He sounds like a typical teenage boy."

130

"But Daddy, he's twenty-four!"

We both stop and watch the word "Daddy" sparkling in front of us, a little Christmas tree ornament
dangling in midair.

EPISODE SEVENTEEN

Emily and Angel

I think about Angel in New York. Is he wrestling with thoughts of me? Waiting for me? I am not in love with Angel. But I wear my sunglasses when I am with him because he is stunning; I can't stop looking at him, and he would be embarrassed. I want to kiss his hands, lick his throat, and stroke him under his shirt. In the beginning I snuck my secret glances at him and waited for him to notice me looking. At first it seemed I was waiting for him all the time. Sometimes the waiting is for nothing. Sometimes he doesn't show up. Sometimes he asks me to leave. Sometimes we are just there. He sleeps like an angel, too, and I worry over him like a nurse. And sometimes we are like two bookends. Alike. Opposite. Holding up all the volumes of our two brief life histories.

He hates it when I tell him stories of my life. He wants to tell me everything that has happened to him. But I know he thinks I believe mine are more exotic, that I am bragging. Well, so what? So is he. He wants me to be still, to absorb his stories, his life. The same way I take in his semen, his information, his DNA. I'm sorry, I interrupted your storytelling. I should just shut up. But it's too late. I have interrupted him, and also told him too much.

When Angel calls me in Paris, I realize it is also his voice that seduces me, not just his face, his neck, and his mouth. His voice crawls under my skin like a crab in the sand. But while his voice burrows into me, his words bounce away. We volley our sounds back and forth, like tennis pros. Score. Love. Game.

But something has shifted in me while in Paris. Maybe I really was just looking for my father. Now Angel waits for me. He accuses me of rejecting him. "You shut me out of your life. Like a door slamming in my face."

"Are you angry?" I ask.

"Beyond."

"How far?"

"How far? I don't know...you changed everything, we were making plans...then? Nothing...you don't even call me to say you've changed our plans...or your mind..."

I like the power of making him mad. I used to avoid it, I thought he'd leave. Now I think he should leave.

"Well, I had to come to Paris, to see my father."

"Yeah, your mother told me but, please, I've made my own excuses for you...besides, what father? Since when did you acquire a father? And what's with this 'Emilia' bullshit?"

"Then you're not angry?" I ask tentatively.

"Yeah, no, I dunno…you...you're wasting my time... I don't have time for this bullshit…" Your precious life slipping away, Angel, I think, while he goes on, "I don't want to waste another minute of my time waiting for you, or talking to you, or whatever."

But here you are, Angel, in the skin of my mind, aggravating as a grain of sand. Maybe you will become a pearl and I can add you to a string of lovers. "Former lovers," I say out loud.

"What?"

"Nothing, I was just thinking out loud...I have to go..."

"Where...where are you going?"

"Maybe a restaurant, I'm hungry, I think I'll go to a restaurant..." Give me a menu. Okay, this is what you serve. This is how much it will cost. And when I am done, I will pay you, and our relationship is over. The transaction is clear. You on one side of the table and me on the other.

Give me a restaurant. Not this.

Not this. That is what our philosophy instructor tells us. I share a class with other women in their twenties and we are attempting a new "philosophy" on "Life." "Not this," the professor assures us, the madness is not "I." It may be me, but not "I." "Not this, not this" we are instructed to remind ourselves so as not to get distracted by *me*. "If not this then what," my friend asks the philosopher, "what about orgasms?" And she acts out an orgasm, crying out "Not this! Not this!" and we laugh. The professor frowns, "Philosopher amateurs, philosopher whores," and, we query further, "If not then, when?" Obviously, her look tells us, we've missed the point. Not surprising for philosopher whores; we both miss and get a lot.

I once explained to Angel, then, that I am not in love with him, that I am practicing being in love. I am torn between Angel, there, and the real thing, the "I" not the *me*. He says, "I don't buy that Philosophy 101 shit. So you're just practicing? Fine, let's go practice." And we had sex.

I've never heard him like this Angel, now, on the long- distance phone call: plaintive, wanting, even poetic. "You still 'practicing' on me? What're you, shooting cans in the air like your mom's lovers, or are you just cleaning the gun? I dunno, first you were innocent, now, I dunno, you're tougher than I knew."

Two days later, I receive a card from Angel. I like having a small drama of my own to share with Eric and Alec. The card shows a big heart carved from a sandy beach, presumed to be Rockaway, and inside it announces "I miss you!" The note reads:

Em (or should I say Emilia)

I feel like a piece of your puzzle, but like a brown piece from the middle. I want to be a defining piece, like the sky, or an edge piece.

I imagined myself your "horizon," but now you reject me. You act like I am trying to control you. Well, what if I am? If you rebel, is it for your own good? Well, okay. Go ahead. You define the terms of engagement. Can you do that? Are you mature enough? I am listening. I will negotiate. Yes, I'd prefer everything on my own terms, but I will settle. Do you want me to beg. All right then, here: "I beg you. Please, I want you. See? I look at other women, but I am only pretending to want them; all I want is you, with them I am faking." How is that?

Signed, *Angel*

It's implausible for me to imagine him painstakingly carving each letter in the sand and harder still from the page. I suspect he had one of his other girlfriends stroking his back while he is writing it and teasing impatiently for him to pay attention to her: "come on, Angel, come back to bed..." and him slyly smiling at her while he licks the envelope closed. More likely she wrote it for him, leaning the card on his back while stroking him too. On the phone, Angel continues to try to get through to me. "Emily, *Emilia*, why are you suddenly cold to me?"

"Cold? How can you say that? I'm your girlfriend, aren't I?" I say sarcastically.

"I don't know, I thought you were, I don't know, infatuated, didn't you say so?"

"Once...but..."

"But? Now I'm hooked, baby! I don't want to lose you!"

"Me, and who else, A? ...things change...I changed...my life changed. I found my father. And he needs me now."

"But how do I get you out of me?" he asks, "Surgery? Philosophy? What about me?"

Me, always me. The first two letters of the word "men."

Alec is right. Finally the act of keeping, holding, letting go -- not this! not you! -- exhausts us. I made the mistake of crossing over, from treating Angel like an object to thinking of him as my lover, and now the bridge is washed out and so am I. And where are you now, Angel? Under my skin, like a splinter. And I'm not even in love with you.

"I gotta go...I have to go see my father. He's dying." It's the first time I say the words out loud, and they hurt.

The night before I'd left New York for Paris, I asked my mother to write to me, write to me about what it's like to be in love, what is it? She wrote me a note.

"It's chemistry, she writes. It's the weird transformation that happens when we grow up, when left on our own, old enough to go on without adult supervision, old enough to have periods and orgasms and children and yet still innocently be biased, no, not biased, hamstrung, by ideas about romance, passion, sex, and how it's all supposed to mix together like biscuit dough, or better, like a walnut-encrusted sweet syrupy doughy soft bun, served on Sunday morning with a great cup of coffee and the *New York Times*. And, oh the best part! No cares! Hah! Only in our dreams! While we're busy reading Arts and Leisure, the little dream is coming apart at the seams. But don't let me discourage you."

Right, Mom.

It was funny growing up watching the men in my mother's life jousting for her attention. In her own plain, stout way she let them knock themselves out while she went serenely about her business of working, writing, raising me. I want a man like that. Jousting for me. Suited up in leather and metal. Beating up other men. Then coming home to me, no, not home, to my bed, all sweaty and smelly, tearing off his epaulets and unlacing himself, all the while gorged and steaming like the jungle and staring deep into my eyes. And me? Sweet and smelling of lavender, and waiting, full of mystery, and certainty. All succulent juice and tangles, like a honeysuckle bush. And never thinking about eight.

EPISODE EIGHTEEN

Emily

I confide in Alec, "A friend told me that he craved a girl who is his pal. And also a woman who keeps her mystery. I'm neither and I'm both."

Alec considers this for a moment. "Then you will confound men and they will try to possess you."

"And be rid of me. They don't know what to do with me."

I pause to contemplate this. "I know what to do with them; I have finally figured it out. 'Just fuck me,' I say now. They don't believe me, though. They think I want other things. Oh, I see. I am supposed to get angry now. Scream at you 'Get out. I don't ever want to see you again!'"

"So you don't scream?"

"I don't scream. I just turn away and say 'Next.'"

"You are a girl after my own heart. And such a pal."

"There are so many opportunities!"

"To...?"

"To see another one! Rise! Then fall. To watch the whole drama, my own private theater."

"And you are such a great audience..."

"I am! I hold my breath! I gasp! I applaud. Nice job. Good review. I'll send my friends. Next?"

"You're hopeless. You treat men the way I treat women. And men, come to think of it." I suspect he is flattering me. "But I know you scream when you are coming."

We laugh.

"You really are my daughter, after all, such a slut." And he holds my hand to his face and kisses the back of it, like a knight a lady. "Just be careful."

Alec tells me of his encounters on the street, mostly with men and prostitutes. One night after leaving the hospital, I decide to try it. A handsome man, an American, I think, passes me and looks at me from the corner of his eye. I stop and turn and watch him. He is alone. But I move too fast. With a fake French accent I say, "Since I've troubled to follow you I should at least offer to buy you a drink." He is in the middle ground somewhere between intrigue and horror. "Where are you from, mister?"

"Texas, the US."

He is not sure where to look, and I continue blurting, but I am selling fast; he is getting away.

"My girlfriend..."

"Ah la petite amie."

I fail in my hilarious mission and when I tell Alec he says, "So now you are a hunter too. It sounds like I must give you some lessons."

That night I walk again. I meet a man -- how simple it is. Just crossing the street. How does a conversation start? "Hello. Nice night. It is a nice night, isn't it. The traffic here is always bad." Good, good. It doesn't really matter what is said; what matters is an instinctive will to survive. This person is not an ax murderer.

So it happens. We wait. We cross. We speak. We stop in a café. He is not gay, he is a straight man, but then, something else I don't comprehend.

"I practice abstinence," he confesses.

Abstinence. It is an interesting word. As in absent, or stingy. I am perplexed. "This is so... interesting... so strange.. I thought abstinence was an accident..." Not a discipline.

So I meet a man, a handsome man, on a street

corner. How strange. Life's odd little road maps. Go here, then there, then? Don't go anywhere, just stop. Wait. Cross. Talk. And then I remember that for a few moments I forget to worry about Alec. Sometimes I think I am always in a state of forgetting, then remembering. Forget Angel. Remember Alec. As if I am a load of laundry, always either dirty or clean.

I amuse Alec, my mentor, with my hopeless encounters. I am becoming attached to Alec, and think I might love him.

I hit the road. To hell? To heaven? Will I meet an archangel? Or a satanist. So far I am lucky. Just your average neurotic male, no psychopaths. Oh, I can see me falling for a psychopath. Just my type. Lie to me, Baby. Tell me all the lies I always wanted to hear. Then forget you told them to me. Forget they were promises. Forget we had plans.

Why does this make me think of Alec, my father? I wonder if that is what I am looking for, is that what Alec is looking for, too? The killer lover. Not "la petite morte." La grande. The real one. Yes? Oui ou non? But the psychopath that will kill Alec emerged silently, carrying a positive face, not an ax -- a deadly swindler.

EPISODE NINETEEN

Alec

The next day is Sunday and Alec is watching an American preacher blast forth on the television. "Let me lay down in green pastures."

Alec my father pauses and reflects a little more on his past.

"I remember a woman in my life. A buxom, perfumed woman, much older, larger than life woman. She lived in the Negresco Hotel with her rich industrial husband."

"Madame Enid," I interject.

"Yes, Enid. Do you know about Enid?" He looks at me curiously.

"I have her diary."

"Her diary? Oh, I guess Eric gave it to you. That's good. She wrote me many letters, and the diary. Eric always kept these things for me; he's good that way, he's the repository of the things in my life that other people keep... letters, pictures...there in a suitcase, in his apartment."

"Yes. He gave me the suitcase, too."

"Yes, he should give you the suitcase."

"Yes, Eric has given me the suitcase. I opened it. I'm sorry. I should have asked." Or waited, I don't say out loud.

"No. No, that's good, I wanted Eric to give it to you. And I'm glad you didn't wait to open it."

I think about the contents, the faded linen suit, the kid gloves, the picture of Giselle in a dainty red dress and matching red shoes. Giselle was beautiful, and though her happiness was apparent in her vivid crinkly smile, it was also brittle, like a delicate crystal glass that was sure to break in the wrong hands. I relate them to the man in front of me. How our lives come down to just a few quaint objects, and then we are gone, and then the objects take on another meaning.

"That impressed me. No one lives in the Negresco Hotel, but she did, and she was hugely attracted to me, and I thought she was sensuous. This minister reminds me of a story she told me. She was attending a friend's funeral and heard the pastor repeat, 'Let me lie down in green pastures.' She described how her mind took off in an alarming sexual fantasy about screwing me in a pasture, right there at her friends' funeral. All I could think to myself was, 'No! no! Please don't make me lie down in a pasture. Get me a doorway, a stairwell, give me concrete! Live music! Surprises. Coins! Noise! Confusion. Either complete abstinence or total indulgence, but please, just please. Don't make me lie down in the grass."

"Did you love her?"

"Who?"

"The larger-than-life perfumed lady. Enid."

"Love her? Well, I kept her company, and she kept me. For a very brief and intense summer, and then over a long time, I saw her once in a while, when I needed money. I think she took up with a series of busboys from the private beach after that. The concierge confided in me once, as though I were really *her* guardian. He thought perhaps it was for her own good that someone, certainly never her husband, would intervene and save her from herself. I never thought she needed saving. She just needed young men to rub her fat breasts brown from the sun and hold her hand while she sniffled about how her husband never made love to her anymore."

"Do you want me to read to you from her diary?"

Alec ponders this darkly for a moment, then brightens.

"Yes. Yes, I'd like that. Will you bring it with you tomorrow?"

Every day now when we part, we make a plan for the next day, not sure how many more next days there are going to be.

That night I read the diary and try out voices with Eric before we decide on the one I will use when I read it to my father in the morning. I veer between breathy Marilyn, an austere Greta, and a masculine Marlene.

"That's the one," Eric applauds, "the one that is co-quettish and dramatic."

EPISODE TWENTY

Enid

Madame

I greet Alec with a peck on the cheek; we make small talk as I prop him up on his pillow and make sure he has what he needs, juice, water, blanket over his toes, the nurse's call button.

When I open the diary, it smells of faded perfume and dust and I imagine Madame Enid fading into the next life the same way. When I start to read I quickly abandon the artificial voice; I recognize a true picture of Alec in her diary and I want to give it to him straight. I also see a woman blossoming through the weight of her love and attraction to my father and I want her to be recognized one last time through her own words.

June 29

When I met you, Alexandro, I thought I had dreamt you… I was the frog kissed by the beautiful prince…when we made love …the first time…I thought "I made this man child up"…whole cloth…you are the boy I wanted when I was fifteen… and now after all these years you emerge…like a boy Venus from a shell in the sea… I succumb to thoughts of you…you are so coquettish… you make me feel like a young flirt …like myself again… who conquers whom…who conjures who… who wins and who gives in?

Unlike my encounters with my husband… with him I am either helpless or an emotional tyrant… both… so I am prepared to win or lose with you. It is time for me to surrender.

In many ways you are my fabulous brooch…a centerpiece in conversations with other women… I remember playing that role myself, with Monsieur H…years ago, guileless, at his side. "Where are you taking the child today?" shopkeepers would ask…it didn't matter that I was the child… the adornment. So obviously different from the man…he was the whole person like themselves. I was the other…enchanted and enchanting… without a past to reconcile … only a future that spoke of beautiful gifts and wonderment for the man lucky enough to decorate himself with me. Now you decorate me…I wear you like a fancy piece of jewelry… or a shield? But that is the nature of adornments… "See the badge of my success. There. Now you can't touch me because I am armored by my prowess. Here, proven by my badges."

Alexandro, you are a wonderful lover…

"So you're a wonderful lover," I note, a little sardonically.

"So she said."

July 1

The first time I saw you, Alex…oh, you are sinuous, an open secret…a secret cave, too…like a pirate's cave… full of stolen treasure … a pirate, too. Your sly, sensuous body… your seductive smile…your eyes that promise to make magic… chestnuts on fire. Your bare throat…exposed but not revealing. The look, into my own eyes…as if you've already entered me and know your way around…as if my life had been one thing until then and your brief deep gaze into me marked a change…a comma or a semi-colon. Call me!

July 3

You surprise me at first…such a young man…your aggressive ardor is like a strong hot wind and it startles me … That first time…well, it is the first time we kiss, isn't it…it will be another week before we make love… I am kidding…the first time is raw, passionate sex…yes, that would be more accurate.

I should have realized I have been giving you the

150

green signals to proceed... otherwise why would the young rogue who sits in the bar at the Negresco...drinking nightly with his friends... even think that I...a mature, well, a matron of the Negresco upper class ... hah,hah, I make fun of myself... even consider him a possibility...or even notice me.

That first time...I like the way you convince the concierge to let you deliver my clothes to my rooms...yes... I admit to mixed feelings when I open the door to find you there...have I been flirting with you... yes, yes, I suppose I have been...more obviously than I realized.

"Is your husband out?"

He wouldn't be returning for hours.

"Well, yes, but just for a few minutes." I lie that time because I am afraid to let you in...afraid of your ardor, my own...when you lean toward me and kiss me on my mouth and press your hard young supple body into mine... I push you away, confused, do you remember? I know what I am about to lose, my safety... and you are my biggest risk... my heart is in danger.

"No. No. Not like this, not now." My desire is tempered by my trepidation.

You apologize for not being more polite...but you do not apologize for kissing me.

"But I am much older than you."

"I like older women."

And I cannot forget your ardor... I make up my mind

to have you when my husband is scheduled for business in Paris.

It is not difficult to signal to you in the bar...every evening I bring a can of food for the fat tomcat who lives the leisure life of "le chat du café" and you become part of the ritual. "Big pussy" you call "le chat" ...and then you look me in the eye as you say it.

You are always surrounded by friends, and there is a girl, a plain, pleasant-looking girl, a young American woman, a travel writer, the waiter tells me...yes, I've inquired about you and your friends. The American girl is always nearby... hanging off to the side... not really with you or with the others...she is like a shadow rather than like a real person...your shadow. Your friends call you Alex and she calls you Alec. I will never call you Alec. I never call you by name.

"Ouch." I feign pain.

"What?" Alec looks at me quizzically.

"She's referring to my mother, isn't she?" I realize I have to hide the diary from Jante.

"Are you ready for me now?" I ask you, over the can of cat food smelling salty like the sea and the big pussy.

You shoot a brief glance at your friends at the bar, and the American girl especially notices your glance...but her look back to you... the question in her eyes doesn't really

*penetrate you…though it tries to, it goes unanswered…
as if she is only a surface on which your own light falls…
and maybe that is why she is just like your shadow. Maybe
she is.*

"Just give me a few minutes," you say.

*Then I become self–conscious… I am sure the entire
room can read my mind…and I want to run away from
this encounter…from its aftermath.*

I think about Jante and how wrong my father was
for her; she is as loyal as an oak tree and as strong as he
is weak.

*"No. No. You'd better not, someone will know you're
coming to see me."*

"Don't worry. Don't worry." You reassure me.

I am torn between yes and no. Push me pull me.

"Don't tell anyone," I beg. Again, you reassure me.

*In my bed I am free… to explore you… the full range
of my desires with you.*

*As I clasp your back, I cry out, "What will I do with
you?"*

*"Keep me," you implore as your cream bursts into me.
"Keep me."*

Yes…but how…I wonder.

July 7

"*Will you come to my room?*"

"*Yes. Will you kiss me?*"

You kiss me... on my hand, on my mouth, on my neck, in my doorway...and your eyes find me in my secret garden...and strip my leaves from me until I remain just a blossom...ready for picking...at my age!

"*Yes. I will come to your room.*" *I don't know where your room is or when I will go, but I promise to go, and I will. I will.*

I dream... no...I am not dreaming...I am not awake... I lie in my bed at the edge... between dark and light this morning... as if I am awake in a dream... and I am in a large deep red circle surrounded by a heavy black background... I am in this inner red circle with you...you are causing me to be in it... it is through you that I can experience the red instead of the black...and I fear for the moment when the red will bleed completely into and through the black...and then what will become of me...where will my outline go... without a frame I will not know where I begin and where I end.

July 12

My life is suspended... between moments I spend with you... moments I spend without you... I am a pendulum.... I am a seedling... you are the wind and the sun and probably also the rain… and me? A kernel of daring and change…

July 13

I am surprised at your command in bed… I call you "el conquistador"… so young and virile I become supple.

"El Conquistador!" I holler hysterically. "Wait 'til Eric hears about that!"

"You think Eric hasn't read this diary a thousand times?" Alec responds wryly. "He probably knows it by heart."

In the middle of the night… you quietly slip into me… I am reminded that you are a boy, after all…and I am an older woman whose arms are open and breasts are large… when you spend yourself inside me you are like a child bringing home his fears and cares to mama…or a favored cat who has thoughtfully left today's catch at my doorstep … when you leave, my bed is immense and empty.

In addition to your je ne sais quoi elegance, your sub-tle coarseness embarrasses me…I cannot make our affair public. And despite your edgy coarseness…which I rub up against like a hungry, flirting cat, your skin is smooth and hard as glass … you are genteel.. I don't know what you do for a living. I suspect it is secretive, shady, maybe il-legal… maybe it is me. My husband would be appalled

155

or laugh…not at my affair…only at my class crossing…
    "You're slumming," he would say, and laugh cruelly.

Despite Madame's pallid description of my mother I am beginning to like Enid. And je ne sais pas, what do I know about love, I am only reading its manual.

July 17
    I deliver my note to the concierge this evening… I am ill at ease …as if I am a spy leaving a small time bomb in the hotel's mailbox. "For Msr AM--" I am sure the bell-boy… the guests and the delivery men… pause to watch me cross the lobby… I feel naked in my indiscretion.
    "Oui, Madame…" With one vigilant eyebrow lifted, the concierge tastefully… discreetly… lifts the corner of the little explosive and places it in your mail box… as if it is something distasteful…not a dangerous package.
    "Alexandro…
    "Je ne comprends pas cette affaire. J'aime tes yeux, ta bouche, tes mains…. Je suis amoureuse de toi, je suis une vielle folle pour toi. My husband is away. My door will be open for you tonight."
    It is open…it is open all night…but you don't come… I'd forgotten this side of passion…the mad side…as if someone has laced the candy with poison.
    I dream the concierge has come… he tells me that you will be along in a moment… I awake and listen…to the

lift… footsteps. I dress and descend to the lobby…la vielle folle. Crazy old fool! I remind myself … I return to my floor… quickly… because I think I've heard the other lift ascend… I fear you are on it and I will miss you…and what will they say when Madame shows up in the lobby or in the bar at 2 a.m.…hurriedly dressed, a hat askew only to disguise her rumpled hair…so unlike Madame.

July 18

I sleep and wake to hear my door opening, but it is a dream…I awake again my mind raging around each sound… the lift?… a footfall? until dawn and I have to admit. You are not coming…poison candy…that is what I eat for breakfast today.

In the morning I spy the little envelope, sealed and virginal in your mailbox. So you didn't even know you were invited to my splendid private party. And now my husband is due from Paris…and my door will be locked.

"Oh, too bad." I am now into the little drama.

Alec acknowledges, "Hmm, I guess I was a disappointment."

July 23

"I am so much older than you."

"I like older women," you remind me. "I like you."

And I am an old fool, in love…for the first time in so

157

many years…did I ever love my husband this way…was he ever so desirable…?

July 25

I finally visit your chamber for the first time… I have to reach your room through a back stair and find it on the third landing at the rear of the hotel. I am struck by its simplicity…the opposite of my own with its pillows… mirrors and throws… its photographs and paintings pushed into piles along the walls… its decadent peeling paint… its glorious view of the Promenade des Anglais. And the sea… the mother sea… gently rocking the shore to sleep at night or rousing it with a riotous party of waves… ever present, forever unconditional.

There is little that is personal in your room. Your white linen suit hanging over a chair… a pair of exquisite brown kid gloves…a photograph of a pretty, laughing woman in a red dress.

"My mother," you explain. "She died when I was twelve." You gaze at the photo for a brief shadowed moment and put it face down on the bedside table.

"Giselle," I say. "The photo of her. May I…?"

"Yes, of course, you will have it all, my little suitcase of memories. Emilia, it is all I have to give you."

"I was just beginning to learn about sex then." And you take me into your arms and kiss me briefly. "I was introduced by a woman… an older woman. She was my mother's best friend." You take my hand and place it seductively on your man's thing. "She put her hand on my little cock and opened my pants and released it from the safety of its child's drawers -- and she put her mouth full around it. It shot off warm pudding — delicious, she said it was — a little stream of baby juice, she called it."

When you look into my eyes with your angelic -- excuse me, devil may care, maybe devil eyes … I don't know which to expect. The devil. The innocent. The passerby. I can't know yet which role you will accept. Or impose on me.

"You like that story of your first time; everyone hears it," I tease.Alec just looks at me and purses his lips as if to say, "You're mocking me."

August 10

It is weeks since I've seen you. I don't call your room anymore…that plain Jane stays with you… she even answers your phone… I am left to either chance… or little incendiary devices like the envelope…please call me.

August 11

After not seeing you… you make it up to me…in the lift…in the stair. "Quiero contigo." You even sly my private phone number from me. "How did you do that? You must be a spy. Only my husband knows this number. And now you do too."

And it slipped out between my lips and before I knew it I was giving away my own private state secret. "How did you do that? You really know how to get things, secrets out of a woman. Don't you?"

With you I am full… of light and soft corners…without you I am dark and sheer…when I wake up my morning is something I open into… I used to avoid the day… as if I were an old house… my shutters closed, my curtains drawn. … I am beginning to glow in the dark…. If I grow any brighter I will keep my husband awake all night with the blinding light…or I will burst into flames.

"Here it is," I say, "the part about the green pastures."

August 13

"He maketh me lie down in green pastures, he restoreth my soul…."

The pastor's words are meant to solace my friend's mourners… instead, my mind inserts me into the image and "He" becomes he…becomes Alexandro, becomes you, "he maketh me lie down into green pastures that surround me...your legs, your hands, your feet, your tongue are green... they entangle me like a sinuous vines...your eyes are my chestnut masters.

"Golly, she's made you into a god."

"It's fun to be worshipped...especially? When you get paid for it."

August 15

We have a date...it is a holiday...we are going for a drive. Along the Corniche...away from the Negresco... perhaps find a room on the way. You have my number, but you do not call...two hours after our appointment, my husband returns to find me suspended in a terse, angry net. I do not understand... I am older and richer...I am supposed to be in control here...but I forget...between a man and a woman the woman is always the lower caste. No matter the circumstances.

August 16

"Princesa," you call me.

Princess...no one has ever called me Princess...not my father...not my grandfather...never my husband. Enid... that's the only name my husband has ever called me ...not even Enid Dear.

"Princesa." Princess... I remember that ... when you

161

hurt me… a result of your youth …such excuses I make for you! You leave me … unattended…unflattered…all your other interests of the moment…women… I don't know what… keep you away.

I take pride… in my learning … in my maturity… but now I structure my time to accommodate you… how willing I have become to inconvenience myself… for you! I finally give myself over to love… yet I still find myself doubting the capitulation. Coyness…finally thrown overboard… and I am soaked to the skin… clinging to the lifeline… my life jacket is at sea. And so am I.

Then your words … straighten me out. Your words… my biggest hope…your voice, my great solace…your simple phrases, designed to heal me: "Let go of the bad; just hold on to the good." (After you have hurt me.) "There will be many nights. Many, many nights." (After you have stood me up.) "There will be many days. Many, many days." (After you have stood me up again.) "You want to control everything." (After you didn't call me.) Only when you need money are you silent.

August 22

We meet at the carousel in Cannes…you do not like it…you hate the way it continues on its stupid sentimental circling journey… going nowhere…around and around…spinning too fast yet getting nowhere…everyone on it grinning stupidly… except the few small children who cling to their horses' necks, terrified... you identify with them...trying to hide their fear from their grinning parents...even from the horses.

I confess to you that in secret, I ride the carousel... Alone...every February, or at the latest, March.

"It is how I break from the winter darkness."

I ride and wear that lovely grin...alone and free... going nowhere. I forget all of winter's pain and bleakness. In slow motion, we all ride as if dead... in heaven...the horses themselves caught up in hideous grimaces, their bodies forever trapped in ecstatic tension...fleeing yet frozen... their riders' dopey grins caught like drunken children.

You humor me... but I can tell you are at least perplexed... at worst ashamed... even appalled... at the thought of the "grande dame" riding a merry-go-round at all...no less alone...no doubt in some useless quest for innocence. I suspect you privately vow never to make this kind of spectacle of yourself and will forget this image of me as fast as you can.

August 23

I spent my youth... a girl... a girl person...with looks and appeal... and intelligence. If only there had been a smarter way!... to use that basic material... to become something greater than the "grande dame"... the older woman...the successful wife. If only the view of the Mediterranean Sea outside my window had been a view of myself instead... that I held that view in my own hands...instead of viewing myself through the view of the sea as a mirror for my lovers...my husband...anyone who cared to look.

That is how it has been this summer...when you are here I am reborn... when you are not I am abandoned... waiting...like an unwanted child. I don't understand... your forgetfulness, your neglect... neglect of any kind is heart-twisting...I know...I learned from my husband... I've never gotten used to it...after all these years. Only Alexandro moves me from this stasis...but when Alexandro is gone too, I will be lonely. I am like one of those carousel horses... caught up in a hilarious grimace... frozen... hopelessly going around in circles.

I hang on to you, Alexandro, at least the thought of you. You are becoming so much a thought... so little a reality, as if you too are one of those wild plaster carousel horses...your mane perpetually out of place... your face forever fixed in a sterile, frozen wildness. And the reins in my hand little more than dress ribbons... of no use harnessing you in.

Madame's last entry is dated a year later, September:

Ce soir...I was eating in le Rotunde and a gentleman there reminded me so much of you...there dining avec son jeune fils and sa femme... she was plain and spied me watching her husband... their son was si beaux...like a petit fils Alexandro. I regret I was not able to meet the gentleman... he was so like you he made me ache...it is just as well... men like him...like you...just tear my seams apart... I hope you are well.

Amor, Enid.

P.S. Write to me when you need money. I can weasel some away from my husband, he is good for that.

P.P.S. Alexandro, My husband is home most of the time now...he wants to move to the country, he is getting old.

I AM SENDING YOU MY DIARY IN CASE I DIE BEFORE MY HUSBAND DOES. Love, Enid.

"Daddy?" I ask. I pause and take a deep breath. "Will you call me Princesa?"

EPISODE TWENTY-ONE

Unnamed

As I read this to Alec, the yellowed pages are pungent with age and Enid's perfume faintly surrounds us like an old woman whose skin lets off an unmistakable aroma of time, hope, and opportunity past and lost.

"I remember, sort of, reading all this before. But I can't remember the adventures she described; it's as if she were having an affair with someone who looked like me, a stand-in for me, but not me. But she also spent money on me. She didn't have much of her own, but she could always contrive something or another from her husband. I think he had someone in Paris and they each went to some effort to hide each other's game to protect their own."

"She gave you money?"

"Well, sometimes cash – which I preferred-- but often it was more indirect. Say I needed something. Clothes, to repay a debt. Or to further my 'career'..."

"You had a career?" I almost choke on the question.

"Well, oh god, that's an awkward question. Sort of. Well, let's just say I made a living." Another pause. I was finding it interesting to pay attention to Alec's pauses; these were his own moments of self-revelation.

"Well, it would have been difficult for me to support a family, you understand. Don't you?" He asked this of me in the most plaintive voice I had yet heard him conjure up. I think he meant it. It was honestly not within his imagination to create a reality where he would be a responsible member of anyone's family, never mind the patriarch responsible for it. And then again, Jante never told him about me.

"So then."

I ask Alec, my father, about the woman he left my mother for. For a few moments, my father, his head wistfully resting on the hospital pillow, looks perplexed. Challenged, then enlightened. "Oh yes, B..." Long pause.

"I'd almost forgotten her."

Another pause as he gazes out the window. A nurse sallies up to his bedside. "Time for another swallow of your favorite juice, Señor..."

"Ah, the cockroach slime …"

"B. She was smart. Successful. Well off. Educated. I was impressed with her education. I liked that she thought I was a clever boy. I thought at first, I don't know what I thought... you know, I never really thought about this until just now, why've you asked? Never mind. Why did I leave your mother...well of course she wasn't your mother then, you know, she left me for the States without telling me she was going to have a baby... that was her special punishment to me, I guess for B..."

I think it highly unlikely that Alec my father would have foregone his lifestyle had my mother stayed and borne me in Europe, but I don't say anything. I can't imagine Alec my father bouncing his cherubic baby girl on his knee, except for the briefest maybe, politest moment before swiftly handing me back to whosoever's arms would embrace me.

"...I thought B would provide all the things missing in my life. Not an unusual foundation for many affairs, true?"

"No." I had to suppose that was true. "Like...?"

"Well, class. Education. Financial security. A future. All the things Jante -- well, all the things I, my parents, my family, *your* family -- sometimes we possess them and sometimes we toss them away, but never really have, or can keep."

Another long pause. "But then..." I am brought back; during Alec's pause I reflect on those missing elements of our lives, all the things that represent permanency. All the aspects of other people's lives that look like a berth in the storm to us, not just the flimsy anchors we throw over from time to time to brake (or break?) the legs of our journeys. "...too suddenly, I realized, she wasn't it..."

"And now, just now, I have to realize, she was just a key...one that opened something locked inside me. I felt trapped...I'm sorry, I know Jante is your mother and you love her, and I loved her too, in my own obtuse way, but I did feel trapped." Imagine had I been born already, Jante, me, we all would have been trapped,

"I needed a way out...B presented it..."

B saved us all.

Alec pauses again, a long time, and gazes out the window. I hope he appreciates, as I do, my willingness to sit, openly, passively and passionately, at the side of his dying body while he speaks freely maybe for the first time and definitely, defiantly for the last time in his life.

"Anyway, I felt trapped. And needed some nugget, something shiny, to grasp. Like a fish on a hook, I guess..."

"Or a brass ring."

"Yes, whatever, like a crow, attracted to shiny objects, just something, anything. Just get me out of here..."

I listen, but I want to protest. If I were Jante, my mother, I would know exactly what I wanted to say now, what I've wanted to say all these years. But I'm not Jante, I am Em, and don't say anything. And now you, Alec, my father, are telling me everything, whatever comes to your mind, whatever questions I demand an answer to. I am not your daughter. I am your tape recorder. Your priest. Your other self.

"So, did she change your life?"

"Course not. Within months I was disillusioned. She was just another trap. And I just made her angry."

Now I seek the escape of the window, looking there instead of at Alec.

"How, uh, how," I hesitate to ask. "How did you feel about my...about Jante?"

"Jante?" His response is surprisingly quick and sure. "Jante? Jante was good. She was good for me, at least. She was steady, a steady presence, she was reassuring. And she made no demands on me. She was just there. And she taught me to speak American English. I think I was more comfortable around Jante than with almost anyone I've known, except of course Eduardo, my uncle, Eduardo." He peers at me quizzically. "And now, of course, you."

Alec smiles at me, and I realize it is the first time I have seen him smile. And I am not altogether comfortable with it; it is like a handsome watch that turns to face you as if to say "See, I can tell time, too."

"We would just be sort of in the same place at the same time, watching the same things, not talking much, not laughing together much, though there was one time when we fought over the mechanical shutter in our room at the Splendid Hotel...up no down! down no up!"

"Yes, yes she told me about that."

"...and we laughed so hard and finally Kaput! it was stuck in the middle, so neither of us won. And every time we went out on the terrace we had to bend over to get under the broken shutter, which made us laugh again each time."

"I have a picture of her."

I had wondered if there'd be an opportunity to share this with him, or even if he'd be interested. "Do you want to see it?"

Alec picks his head up now and leans on his skinny arm. "Yes, yes, I'd like to, very much."

He remains like that while I fumble through my

wallet, and when he looks into the photo he seems to be looking for someone he knows, recognizes, but rather it is like he is looking politely at someone else's family photo, like one does when viewing the pictures of a wedding or a birthday party and every one is a stranger.

"She's put on some weight."

"Yes, I suppose she has. She left Manhattan and bought a little house on Rockaway Beach, in Queens. She likes it there; she wanted to be near the water."

I find myself speaking quickly, and just as fast putting the photo away. I don't want him to suddenly not like her; I want to preserve the memories of her that he'd just shared with me.

"She calls it her Riviera of New York City."

"You know," Alec reflects, "as soon as money enters the equation, love becomes the commodity. It loses its innocence, its freedom. It's chained and traded like any other currency. A value is placed, and some gamble on its gain — I love you, and some on its losses -- I hate you. But you know. You have to watch the pageantry of your life. You are the star, the audience, the critic..."

"And the director?"

"No, no, never the director. That's the mistake everyone makes. We think we direct our own pageant... tell our own story, that we get to decide, who does what to whom, when...no, that's the biggest mistake..."

We are getting used to looking into each other's eyes; Alec's brown like chestnuts, but graying and fading.

"My dear...my dear, dear...daughter..."

It is the first time he acknowledges me, Emily, Emilia, as his daughter. His look pierces me like a needle. He reminds me of a tailor, bent over and sewing an old button into cloth that is worn with stitches, and threadbare. His eyes seem to sag, resigned and also relieved. I am the soul who has formed a pillow, and he is the soul who has found his own handmade quilt.

"No, no, we're never our own director..."

We pause, together. We each look outside the other, ourselves, out the window. The blue sky both blurts out the world's goodness and screams out its inconsistencies.

"If we're lucky..."

"Smart?"

"Paying attention... we can see..."

"The pageant?"

"Yes, usually...we see the edges, just stuck in the marrow of the bone..." He looks at me again. "Just try to remember...see? The pageant of your life...it's big... it's wide... and you are your best critic..."

I don't know if he closes his eyes because he is exhausted, or because he has just experienced more intimacy than he knows, can stand. And I am tired, too. And I am not sick and dying. Just trying to find out who I am, through a dying man.

"Daddy?"

Alec opens his eyes for a moment.

"Will you call me Princesa?"

He smiles wanly, pats my hand and closes his eyes again. "Yes, my Princess."

EPISODE TWENTY-TWO

Emily Continued

I feel I am a detective seeking clues to my family's mystery, the mystery of me, or like a gold digger scratching for the shining bead. To my father I am a priest confessor. My mother? She coyly doles out her secrets like a fortune teller revealing one fortuitous card at a time: "Oh, watch out for this one, this one is The Fool." My grandfather — which one? Or should I say my grandfathers. Growing old together like two tree trunks, one keeping Giselle's blue eye, the other her brown. They each embraced Alexandro as if he were their own offspring and abandoned him as if he belonged to the other.

Now that I have met my father, I can put together the puzzle that is myself. One moment, one conversation, one memory at a time I fit the pieces into place: the sky, the house, the children playing. The adults? They are behind closed doors, quarrelling, fornicating, and daydreaming of a better life.

I wanted to get to know my father, but these aren't the facts I wanted to know about. This isn't the father I imagined.

We want our parents to be like shellfish that only come out when we bid them. Instead they have a life of their own, way too much of it.

And who does that make me? Why am I here, now? Have I touched my father's life? There is no more of that penetrating light available behind his eyes. As he lay dying they become translucent, clearing away the rubbish of our everyday world, and opaque. Both all-seeing and no- seeing. Blind and wise, embracing something bigger than our daily life of chores and worries. He does not see faithful Eric, and when he looks at us it is with astonishment as if he has already passed to the other side and we are ghosts.

His skin, too, is translucent -- his chest bared, coquettishly even now, between the bed sheets and the hospital gown. How can we be in the same realm when I can pick up my bag, walk down the street, buy a newspaper and a cup of coffee? I imagine him retreating deeper into his mind, away from the pain, and in there he is floating on a cool, calm lake and the sun's sparkling reflection amuses him and he is at peace. For all I know, he retreats into a nightmare.

Watching my father die gives me the courage to live, to ask as many questions as my mind will give rise to. I just ask Life to, please, give me plenty of time to keep asking, to sort out the fragments.

When he does open his eyes in a singular moment he both sees me completely and dismisses me in the same haunting glance.

Eric remains. Eric has become my uncle, an "uncle in the business" of Alec's life, and now my own. His devotion to my father spills over to me and I am grateful for his gentle, worried gestures, patting Alec's hand, plumping a pillow, covering his feet; his small, fretful sighs.

We don't speak much and when we do it is usually about "your father" "votre père" or just plain "A."

"He was a wonderful cook -- did you know that? Of course not, sometimes I feel we've known you all your life! Well,he went through a period, after the diagnosis, when he cooked nearly every night, experimenting and preparing me a menu when I came in from work, and then he lost interest in food. It was all I could do to get him to eat, and look at him now…" This he would whisper to me so Alec couldn't hear. " …Thin as spaghetti, just wasting away…" And he'd be back to reality, shaking his head, holding Alec's fragile hand. And I'd rub Eric's shoulder and end with a small hug until the nurses came and rolled Alec over for another one of their endless procedures, and Eric and I would leave and just take a walk.

What is that Alec gave back to everyone? A talisman? A shooting star? He is the wish upon a star, not the star itself. He embodies the wish, the pretense of all we hope for and want to be. He figured it out at an early age -- how to be the brooch, the emblem.

I always knew I was part Jante, and part someone else, a mystery guest who hung around the corner of the party intriguing all the invited guests.

"Yes," I say to myself, "I am my father's daughter. I am Alexandro, too. Emilia. Emily. Em. M."

In the end, has he finally become himself? I don't think so. He'll have to come back again to finish up that piece of work. Or go somewhere else to be that. Here, he is Alec, my father, Alex, Alexandro, A.

That night I open the suitcase and take out the linen suit. I put it on. Its crispness is faded, and the collar is deeply yellowed. I roll up the sleeves and pant legs a few inches. I pull my hair into a tight, tight ponytail. In the dim light of Eric's foyer, in front of the grand mirror, I pose and can imagine myself with straw hat and even a silver-tipped cane, strolling along the Promenade des Anglais as if I were Alexandro himself. Polished, smooth and hard, seductive as catnip.

The door opens and in the mirror I see Eric, ashen. Stricken. I turn around and he leans into me and sobs disconsolately, and I know Alec is gone.

When Eric catches his breath he whispers, "I don't know what I'll do without him."

"I'll miss him, too."

"He just won't be here again, ever. I won't have him in my life."

"Eric, before I left him last night, he was afraid, and I put my arms around him and I could feel his heart beating here, against my wrist. Here, feel it, Eric, his heart still beats inside me."

Eric presses his lips to my wrist, and I wipe his tears with Alec's frayed linen sleeve.

"He'll always be here, Eric. And so will I."

I gather Eric in my arms and hold him there in the foyer until his tears stop and I walk him to his room and lay him down and pull a worn, thick quilt up and around his shoulders, like a small child whose feelings are hurt beyond repair.

Paris murmurs outside the apartment. I catch a glimpse of myself in the mirror, the faded linen suit now stained with the last tears Eric will shed for Alec, Alexandro, A, my father, and I realize my Life has just begun.

Going out?